"There's a fire[...] we need to lea[...]"

Lilly looked down at her robe and slippers. "Can't we get dressed first?"

"There's no time," said David. "I want to be out of here before the fire department arrives, so we only have five or six minutes at the most."

"You're talking like they're the bad guys."

"That's exactly what I'm afraid of, Lilly," he said. "Henderson might be masquerading as a firefighter again. We have no way of knowing who to trust." He pointed to her open bedroom door. "Go get your daughter, and let's leave."

David's partner approached the front door as someone knocked. "The fire department got here really quick. It looks like they're doing door-to-door checks."

The locks turned just as David realized what was about to happen. "No! Don't do it."

It was too late. The door flew open with a bang, kicked firmly with a firefighter's boot.

"I just want the woman and the girl," Henderson said from behind his mask. "Give them to me...and I'll let you live."

Elisabeth Rees was raised in the Welsh town of Hay-on-Wye, where her father was the parish vicar. She attended Cardiff University and gained a degree in politics. After meeting her husband, they moved to the wild rolling hills of Carmarthenshire, and Elisabeth took up writing. She is now a full-time wife, mother and author. Find out more about Elisabeth at elisabethrees.com.

Books by Elisabeth Rees

Love Inspired Suspense

Caught in the Crosshairs
Safe House Under Fire

Navy SEAL Defenders

Lethal Exposure
Foul Play
Covert Cargo
Unraveling the Past
The SEAL's Secret Child
Innocent Target

SAFE HOUSE
UNDER FIRE

ELISABETH REES

LOVE INSPIRED SUSPENSE
INSPIRATIONAL ROMANCE

LOVE INSPIRED® SUSPENSE
INSPIRATIONAL ROMANCE

ISBN-13: 978-1-335-40265-3

Recycling programs
for this product may
not exist in your area.

Safe House Under Fire

This edition published by arrangement with Harlequin Books S.A.

For questions and comments about the quality of this book,
please contact us at CustomerService@Harlequin.com.

Love Inspired
22 Adelaide St. West, 40th Floor
Toronto, Ontario M5H 4E3, Canada
www.Harlequin.com

Printed in U.S.A.

And be ye kind one to another, tenderhearted,
forgiving one another, even as God for Christ's sake
hath forgiven you.
—*Ephesians* 4:32

For my daughter, Alys

ONE

"Astrid, will you please come here this minute. If I have to ask again, you'll be grounded until Sunday."

Lilly Olsen rushed around her living room, plumping the cushions, straightening the throws and arranging the magazines into piles. She hated to return from work to a messy home, so she tried to make life easier by keeping on top of things. Juggling her job as bank clerk with parenting a wayward fifteen-year-old daughter was difficult enough already.

"Astrid," she shouted, feeling her patience wear thinner than ever. "It's eight fifteen. You'll be late for school and I'll be late for work." She muttered under her breath, "Again."

"Okay, Mom, you don't have to yell. Why do you always have to yell?"

Astrid appeared in the hallway of their one-story home, wearing head-to-toe black clothing, topped off with a velvet beret. She was apparently now going through a goth phase. This came on the heels of a skater phase and a Japanese cartoon phase. She was clearly struggling to establish her identity, and Lilly had learned to pick her battles carefully.

"You can take off that black lipstick in the car," she said, choosing to ignore the rest of the outfit. "I have some wipes in the glove box."

Astrid flounced past her. "You're such a killjoy."

"Yes, I am," Lilly said, retrieving her keys from a hook on the wall. "And that's a good use of the word *killjoy*, by the way. You have a great vocabulary when you choose to use it."

Her daughter groaned and sighed, picking up her school backpack from the hallway floor and opening the front door. As if the day was set against her, a fine mist of rain was falling. Lilly's perfectly straightened, fine blond hair would now frizz up in seconds.

"Well, let's go," Astrid said with an eye roll. "You were the one desperate to leave."

"Don't you roll your eyes at me, young lady," Lilly said sharply, sounding horribly like her own mother. "I don't know what's gotten into you lately. Did I do something wrong?"

"Um, let me think," Astrid said. "First of all, you gave me a totally stupid name."

Lilly was aghast. "Astrid is a beautiful Scandinavian name. You should be proud of your Swedish heritage."

"Second of all," her daughter said, beginning to check the numbers off on her hand. "It's my sixteenth birthday soon and you haven't organized a thing. You know I want a party."

Lilly pinched the bridge of her nose. "I know, I know. We'll talk about it later, okay?" She ushered Astrid through the door and beeped her car to unlock it. "I've been so busy dealing with a very important client at work that it slipped my mind."

"And third of all," Astrid said, following her mom

down the path, clomping in her heavy black shoes. "I wanted Dad to come visit for my birthday, but you drive him away all the time with your snarky attitude."

Lilly stopped dead, turned around slowly and looked her daughter straight in the eye.

"Is that why you're acting up?" she asked. "Are you upset because your father never comes to see you?"

Astrid avoided her gaze and rubbed an arm self-consciously. "It's been two years, Mom. I barely remember what he looks like."

"And you think I'm the one keeping him away?"

"Yes."

Lilly tried to keep her anger in check. She was the one who had cared for Astrid since babyhood, the one who had borne all of the financial burden and was the sole parent barely coping with the emotional roller coaster of teenage emotions. Lilly's ex-boyfriend, Rylan, had been her high school sweetheart and had reacted badly when she became pregnant at the age of eighteen. She'd wanted to do the right thing and get married, but he was adamantly against it. Instead, he'd abandoned her, gradually lessening contact until finally moving away from their small hometown of Oakmont, Pennsylvania, when Astrid was only four years old. He now lived in California, and Astrid was fortunate if she received a Christmas card or a rushed phone call telling her that she had another new baby brother or sister. Astrid had a total of five half siblings, born from three of Rylan's many girlfriends over the last ten years.

"Your father loves you, honey," Lilly said. "It's just that he has a hard time showing it. I promise that I'll try my very best to get him to come visit. I would never keep him away from you. Never."

Astrid stomped to the car and sat in the passenger seat, scowling. At five feet nine inches tall, she cut a willowy and elegant figure when dressed nicely, but in this macabre and imposing outfit, she appeared intimidating. Lilly wished they were as close as they used to be, when Astrid would offer to plait her mom's hair or paint her nails. In the last year, her daughter had grown into a young woman that Lilly mostly didn't recognize.

"Hi, Mr. Peters," she said, noticing her elderly neighbor walk past with his dog on a leash. "I'm sorry for the Wednesday Addams vibe you must be feeling from Astrid this morning. She's having some trouble finding her place in the world."

Mr. Peters smiled. "She's a beautiful soul, Lilly. And she shines brightly just like her mom."

"You're too kind," she said, walking to her car, the compliment lightening her step. "Thank you."

Astrid was peering intently through the windshield when Lilly settled herself behind the wheel of her compact car. "The guy in that van has been watching our house all morning," Astrid said. "Do you know him?"

Lilly looked at the dark gray van parked across the street, the kind of vehicle often used by utility companies. The man in the driver's seat was immobile, staring straight ahead, wearing sunglasses despite the overcast day.

"I'm sure he's not watching the house," Lilly said, fixing her cell phone into its holder on the dash. "He's probably repairing some damage to power lines or something. There was quite a wind last night."

"I'm telling you," Astrid insisted, as Lilly pulled from the driveway onto their leafy suburban street. "He's been there since six thirty. I thought he was waiting to give someone a ride, but he's been watching us like a hawk. It's creepy."

"How can you get up at six thirty and not be ready by eight fifteen?"

Astrid clicked her tongue. "It takes a long time to look this fabulous."

"That reminds me," Lilly said, leaning across to open the glove box. "Take off that lipstick."

Astrid huffed and pulled out the pack of wipes from inside. "Look!" she said, turning around. "The creepy guy is following us."

Lilly glanced into the rearview mirror. The van was on their tail, driving too close for comfort.

"It's just a coincidence," she said, quashing her fears. "He's probably just going in the same direction."

Astrid dragged a wipe across her mouth. "I don't like it. It's making me nervous."

Lilly's phone began to buzz in its holder and the name flashing on the display was Kevin Lovell, her boss at the bank where she worked in Oakmont.

"I gotta take this," she said to Astrid. "But don't worry about the van, okay?"

Eyeing the clock, she punched the answer button and put her cell on speakerphone.

"Hi, Kevin," she said. "I might be a little late this morning." She avoided looking at Astrid. "My usual routine didn't go to plan."

Kevin's voice was bright and breezy, totally out of character for her usually grumpy boss.

"Don't worry about it, Lilly. If you're still at home, then stay there and don't come into work today. And lock your doors."

"What? Why? I'm on the road already."

"Mom!" Astrid's voice was high-pitched. "That van has gotten even closer. I'm scared."

Lilly touched her daughter's knee. "Hold on, honey. Just give me a minute."

"We have a serious situation here at the bank today," Kevin continued. "A couple of agents from the FBI visited a few minutes ago, expecting you to have started work already. They're on their way to your house, so turn around and go home to wait for them. They should be with you soon."

"I have to drop Astrid at school," she said. "Why do I have to go home? What's going on?"

Kevin was silent for a moment. "The agents said you're in danger."

Lilly exchanged a worried glance with Astrid as her daughter grabbed for her hand. She approached a junction and turned left, intending to double back and return home. She didn't know what was going on, but Kevin's words were chilling.

"Mom, the van is following us," Astrid said, beginning to cry. "He's definitely following us."

A different man's voice was now on the speakerphone, a deeper one.

"Ma'am, this is Agent David McQueen from the FBI. I'm patched into this call in my vehicle. Did I hear someone say you're being followed?"

"You're from the FBI?" Why would the FBI be patched into her call? "We think a van is on our tail. What's happening?"

"There's no time to explain the situation right now," the agent continued. "I'm already in the vicinity, en route to your home. Where are you exactly?"

"I'm on Harewood Avenue, approaching the junction to Filton Road. I'm going back home."

"No!" Agent McQueen's raised tone caused them both to jump. "Stay in your vehicle, keep driving in that general area, don't stop and don't panic. I'll be there in five minutes. I'll find you."

Lilly struggled to keep up with the changing pace of the day. Just a few moments ago, she was arguing with her daughter about lipstick. Now an FBI agent was coming to save them from a danger that she had had no idea existed until now.

"Who is in the van?" she asked.

"I'll be there soon. Remain calm."

"How can I remain calm?" Astrid was squeezing her hand so tight that both their knuckles were white. "I have my daughter with me and she's scared out of her mind." She kissed Astrid's fingers and briefly looked over at her. "I'll keep you safe, honey. I promise."

But then the van on their tail revved its engine hard and lurched forward, touching Lilly's bumper. The car skipped, Astrid screamed and Lilly gripped the wheel with both hands to steady their path.

"Mom! Please do something," Astrid yelled. "Make him stop."

Lilly floored the accelerator and tore around the corner of Filton Road, the car's back end skidding away slightly on the wet asphalt.

"What's going on there?" the agent said, still on speakerphone.

"We're being rammed off the road."

"Take evasive maneuvers," he said. "Do whatever it takes."

"I'm trying," she shouted as the van hurtled toward

them once again. Thinking fast, she swerved onto the wrong side of the road. Fortunately, this residential street was always quiet, and she faced no oncoming traffic.

The van was now alongside them and she noticed the driver's gloved hand sharply yank the wheel. He was intending to ram them from the side.

"Hold on, Astrid!" Lilly yelled.

The crunch of metal seemed to sound forever as the van sideswiped her car, pushing it onto the sidewalk, toward the thick trees that grew there.

"Mom," Astrid cried, now beside herself with fear. "I don't want to die."

"Nobody's gonna die, sweetheart. Not today."

She slowed right down to let her assailant pass and then attempted a hand brake turn. But she messed it up and the car ended up sitting awkwardly in the road, straddling both lanes. Meanwhile, the guy in the van was clearly a much more accomplished driver and spun easily on the asphalt, tires squealing and billowing smoke.

Lilly's hand shook as she put the stick in reverse, desperately trying to turn the car around before the van would reach them. But she messed that up too and couldn't move fast enough to avoid the strike. The driver's side of her car bore the brunt of the impact from the hurtling van. Lilly was jolted sideways with huge force, her head banging on Astrid's shoulder. All she could think about was protecting her daughter. This man was crazy. He wanted them dead.

When the car finally stopped shaking, Lilly leaned across her daughter and opened the passenger door.

"Run, Astrid," she yelled. "Run."

Astrid could barely speak through her hyperventilating. "Mom, no, no, I can't leave you."

"Please, honey," Lilly pleaded, seeing the man exit his vehicle and walk toward them. "You gotta go now. Run to Mr. Peter's house and don't look back."

Yet Astrid seemed frozen, unable to move, unable to do anything except cry out in anguish. Lilly turned to see her assailant move calmly and steadily toward them, gun in hand. The hood on his sweatshirt was pulled up and, with his head slightly bowed, his appearance reminded her of the grim reaper.

"Please don't hurt my daughter," she shouted through the shattered window. "I'll give you whatever you want." She grabbed her expensive cell from the dash, a gift from her parents. "You can take this. It's worth over a thousand dollars." As his hand reached up and removed his sunglasses, she forced herself to look him in the eye. "Please."

That's when she recognized him. "Mr. Berger?" she said, confused. "Why are you doing this?"

This man was her important client at the bank. He had visited in person the previous day, wishing to transfer his bank accounts overseas before returning to his native country of France. She had handled the paperwork, shaken his hand, chatted to him about his family. Why did he now want to kill her?

Mr. Berger pointed his gun at her window, and with the sound of Astrid's screams resounding in the car, a bullet cracked the air.

Agent David McQueen heard the unmistakable bang of a gun being discharged as he raced to the intersection of Harewood and Filton. The car was being driven by his FBI partner, Goldie Simmons, and she had wasted no time in rushing them to the scene with the siren blaring. Through his phone's speaker he had been listening to the screams and cries, but they had abruptly stopped. He prayed they weren't too late.

Goldie tore around the corner of Filton and instantly slammed on the brakes to avoid colliding with a blue compact car blocking the street, a gray van stopped behind it.

"That's our guy," David said, seeing a hooded man in the road, weapon in hand. "That's gotta be Henderson."

He jumped from the car, identifying himself as an FBI agent and ordering the man to lie on the ground. As expected, the suspect turned and fled back to his van without allowing David the chance to get a good look at his face. This guy had been successfully evading arrest for more than ten years and David had a very old score to settle.

"You're not getting away this time," he muttered, pulling out his gun and aiming at the van's tires.

"Help! Help! I think my mom's been shot."

A young girl of no more than sixteen suddenly flung herself from the blue compact and ran toward him, arms flailing, her long black trench coat flapping in the wind. She reminded him a little of his own daughter, Chloe.

David couldn't risk shooting now. He reholstered his weapon and called out to Goldie in the car.

"Stay on Henderson's tail," he said, watching the vehicle race toward the busy road out of town. "You'll have to get to the freeway via Harewood but do what it takes to find the van again. Don't lose him."

"You got it."

As Goldie turned the car and screeched away, David put his hand on the girl's shoulder to comfort her. "Is your mom Lilly Olsen?"

"Yes."

He approached the car and bent to survey the scene inside, bracing for the sight of blood, but instead he saw an apparently uninjured blond woman with a flat palm on her forehead, breathing heavily in the driver's seat. In the other hand she clutched a cell phone, her fingers trembling around the black casing.

"Are you hurt, ma'am? Your daughter said you'd been shot."

She held up the cell phone, her face etched with an expression of pained shock.

"It saved me," she said. "I was holding it in front of my face."

The cell was all smashed up, a bullet lodged in the metal, creating a small hollow as though a tiny volcano had erupted in the center.

Then she seemed to gather her thoughts and remember what was important. "Astrid! Is she all right?"

"She's fine, ma'am. She's right here."

"Please tell me what's going on."

David unclipped the radio from his belt. "I'll request a police car to take us to your home. There's a lot of explaining to do."

David stood and watched Lilly Olsen comfort her daughter in the living room of their home, stroking her hair and holding her hand. The teenager had understandably reacted with shock and distress after their terrifying ordeal, but after twenty minutes of soothing, David was beginning to lose patience. As a father of two grown girls, he had plenty of experience as a parent, and he felt that Lilly was treating Astrid with too much mollycoddling. If anyone knew where that would lead, it was David.

"Miss Olsen," he said. "I appreciate the fact that your daughter needs you, but we have important matters to discuss here."

She ignored him for a few seconds, continuing to stroke her daughter's hair while sitting on the couch. Then she turned to him. "I realize that you're here to help us, but my daughter always comes first, so give me a minute or two, okay?"

David gritted his teeth and glanced exasperatedly at Goldie, who had returned from her chase empty-handed. The van had gotten away, and that meant Lilly remained in grave danger.

"You're safe here, honey," Lilly repeated to Astrid. "And nothing bad will happen now."

David stopped himself from interrupting and contradicting her. It was dangerous to tell teenagers that nothing bad happens in life. It was better to tell them that the world was a cruel place and to give them strong boundaries to mitigate the risk.

Astrid rose from the couch. "I'm going to call Noah and tell him why I'm not in school today."

"No phone calls," David said. "Not until I say so."

Lilly rose also and smoothed down her shirt. "She just wants to make a quick call. There's no harm in that, surely?"

"I said no phone calls."

"You can't stop me calling whoever I like," Astrid challenged. "I'm not in jail."

"No, you're not in jail," David said slowly, reminded of the arguments he used to have with Chloe, the big bust-ups that would result in her storming from the house and spending the evening with her totally unsuitable boyfriend. "But I need you to listen to me and do what I say."

"Who put you in charge of me?" the teenager said, sliding her eyes from David's to her mother's, correctly identifying the weakest link in this scenario. "Mom, can I call Noah?" Her bottom lip wobbled, and she rubbed one eye like a tired toddler. "I just want to tell him I'm all right."

Lilly nodded. "Sure, but don't give him any details about what happened today. Tell him you're not in school because you're sick. Okay?"

Astrid glared at David with a hint of triumph before strutting from the room, and his hackles rose. Disobedience was something he could no longer abide in young adults. As a widowed single dad raising two girls, he'd made the mistake of believing that you could reason with teenagers, that you could give them some freedom and be prepared to compromise. But that was before Chloe ended up in a car wreck with her drunk boyfriend and suffered irreversible brain damage as a result. Prior to the accident, she had gone off the rails, become totally unmanageable, and David blamed himself for her downfall. If only he had set stronger rules when she was younger. If only he'd come down harder. And now Lilly Olsen was making the same mistake.

"Teenagers need a firm hand, ma'am," he said. "Trust me, I know. You shouldn't let your daughter get away with manipulating you."

Lilly's brows crinkled beneath her sleek blond fringe. "Manipulating me? Is that what you think she's doing?"

"Yes, I do. She's got you wrapped around her little finger."

She held up a palm. "Excuse me, Agent… What was your name again?"

"Agent McQueen, but you can call me David."

"Okay, David," she said with a false smile. "You literally just met me, and you know nothing about me, or my daughter, so can I suggest that you mind your own business and focus on the man who just tried to kill me."

David rubbed a hand down his face as Lilly's clear blue eyes bored into his. With her arms crossed and her head slightly tilted, her previously soft features now took on a harder tinge. Her criticism was undoubtedly fair. He had lost concentration, thinking back to times when his own daughter had emotionally manipulated him, just like Astrid had with her mom. At that moment, there was a bigger issue to tackle.

"I apologize," he said, sitting on the couch. "You're right. Let's get to work." He pulled a photograph from a file that he had placed on the coffee table. "Was this the man who attacked you?"

She responded instantly. "Yes, his name is François Berger. He's a wealthy art collector, originally from France but living in Pittsburgh for the last twenty-five years. I've been speaking regularly with him on the phone for the past couple weeks and he finally came into the bank yesterday to transfer his money to a European account. He's moving back to Paris next week." She touched the photo. "He seemed so nice when I spoke with him. Why would he try to kill me?"

David placed the photo back into the file. "His real name is Gilbert Henderson and he's a con man, born and raised right here in Pennsylvania."

"No, that's not possible. This guy has a French accent."

"It's fake. Everything about Gilbert Henderson is fake. We've been trying to catch him for more than ten years, but I gotta give him respect where respect is due.

He's cunning, he's smart and he's always one step ahead of us."

"So where is the real François Berger?"

"Dead."

Lilly gasped. "How?"

"We found him in his chest freezer, probably been there a while. We're doing an autopsy to establish the cause of death, but it looks like a bullet to the head."

Lilly clearly struggled to make sense of this. "But… What… Why?"

"Gilbert Henderson targets wealthy individuals with little or no family," he explained. "He chooses somebody with the same age and characteristics as himself. He then murders them and assumes their identity, before setting out to empty their bank accounts and strip their assets. He does this so quickly and professionally that by the time we're alerted to the crime, he's long gone. And so is the money."

"But I transferred Mr. Berger's money to a legitimate bank in France. They'll have procedures to deal with fraud so you can recover it."

David smiled at her naïveté. "Once the money reached the French account, it was moved again and again via very complex channels. It's now been funneled into countries where we have no financial jurisdiction."

"Everything was in order," she said, her eyes scanning the carpet, perhaps wondering how she could have prevented this crime. "He gave me all the right identification documents and said all the right things. I didn't suspect a thing."

"Don't blame yourself. This is probably the fifth time Henderson has gotten away with this type of fraud. We almost caught him this time when a cleaner reported finding Mr. Berger's body in the freezer yesterday and we suspected Henderson was the culprit. But we were just a few hours too late. The apartment has been stripped of the expensive artwork and all of Mr. Berger's accounts are empty."

"If you know this guy's identity, why not just arrest him?"

"We have no evidence to arrest him."

"What? You must have evidence?"

"*You* are the only evidence we have."

"Me?"

"Yes. Henderson is careful to avoid security cameras, he doesn't leave a trace of himself behind and he leaves no witnesses." David realized that he needed to correct his words. "Actually, that's not true. He can't avoid creating one witness per crime, and that's the bank clerk who performs the money transfers. He deliberately chooses banks where the staff won't have met his victim and he'll then interact with just one person during the entire transaction."

"I thought it was a little strange that he didn't go to our bigger branch in Pittsburgh," Lilly said. "But he said he was spending some time with friends in Oakmont and preferred the friendly service of our small-town office." She shook her head. "I can't believe I was actually flattered by the compliment."

"Con men are usually incredibly charming. It's why they're so good at manipulating people."

Lilly was obviously beginning to understand the gravity of her situation. "You're saying I'm the only person who saw his face while he committed this crime?"

"Correct."

"What about the documents he gave me? I took copies

of his passport and driver's license as part of the background checks."

"Those documents belong to the real Mr. Berger, so they're no use to us."

Lilly was wide-eyed and unbelieving. "Really? I checked them thoroughly and the photographs matched the person."

"Henderson only ever selects victims who already bear a strong resemblance to him, and he'll change his hair, wear contacts and false teeth if necessary. None of the bank clerks have spotted the lie so far."

"What happened to them?" she asked, her voice suddenly shaky. "To the other clerks who were duped like me?"

David glanced at Goldie, reluctant to answer truthfully. He didn't want to scare Lilly even more than she was already and, sensing his hesitancy, Goldie stepped into the silence, speaking softly and with concern.

"The other four clerks were all found dead the day after the crimes. We weren't able to save them in time, but we can help you now. We won't allow any harm to come to you. With your witness testimony, we have enough evidence to finally issue a warrant for the arrest of Gilbert Henderson. We just need to find him first."

"Before he finds me," Lilly said. "Because if I'm dead, then he walks free, right?"

"Right," said Goldie. "But that's why we're here. We won't let him find you."

The color had drained from Lilly's face, and David gently patted her hand, which was cold and clammy. "As soon as Henderson is in custody, you'll be safe. He's worked alone ever since his accomplice was murdered ten years ago, so he's the only threat we need to neutralize."

"What happens now?" she asked him. "Do I have to go into witness protection?"

"Yes, just for a short while."

She put her head in her hands. "What about Astrid?"

"Can she stay with relatives until you return home?"

"No, you don't understand," Lilly said. "Astrid saw this man's face when he attacked us today. Won't that make her a target too?"

David caught sight of his partner's stony expression. This was a complication that neither of them had anticipated, and Goldie led David by the arm into the kitchen.

"Astrid is a witness to attempted murder," Goldie whispered. "She saw Henderson's face during the gun attack and that puts her in the firing line. He'll want her eliminated too. You know he never leaves a loose thread."

The last thing David wanted to do was look after a teenage girl, especially one who would undoubtedly push all his buttons and remind him of his most serious failures as a father. But what choice did he have? Astrid was now in as much danger as her mother.

Lilly appeared in the kitchen doorway. "Astrid has to come with me," she said. "I won't go without her."

David noticed that a bruise was appearing on Lilly's forehead. "I agree. Can you both pack some things? Enough for a week to start off."

"Astrid's not going to be happy," she replied. "She'll kick against it, but please try to understand that she's only fifteen. She's a child."

Chloe had been only a couple of years older than Astrid when the car in which she'd been traveling slammed into a tree and damaged her young brain. She had been just seventeen when forced to learn to walk and talk again, to use a knife and fork, to regret not listening to her father.

"Astrid may be a child," David said. "But she can follow orders and do what I ask. I'd like your support in ensuring she complies with my rules."

He saw Lilly's jaw clench, her nostrils flare. This clearly wasn't going to be easy.

"I'm Astrid's mother, and I'll make the decisions on what rules she follows."

David took a deep breath. "From what I've seen of the interactions between the two of you so far, it doesn't appear that your daughter respects your authority."

"Of course she does," Lilly retorted.

"No, she doesn't. She's willful, disobedient and challenging, and I need her to understand that I don't tolerate backchat, not when your lives are in my hands."

Lilly blinked fast, her dark lashes moving so quickly that he almost expected to feel a breeze.

"You don't have kids, do you, David?" she said.

"Yes, ma'am, I do—two daughters, both now in their twenties. Sarah is a lawyer in Philadelphia and Chloe currently lives in Penn Hills."

Lilly's expression was one of surprise. "And did you demand total obedience from them, as well?"

I wish I had, thought David. *Maybe Chloe would now be a doctor like she planned, instead of residing in an assisted living complex.*

"Let's stick to the current situation here," he said, sidestepping the question. "Go talk with Astrid, pack your bags and we'll discuss details afterward."

Lilly stalked from the kitchen, but not before he heard her mutter under her breath, "Control freak."

David leaned against the kitchen counter. He'd rather be accused of being a control freak than a weak parent. And no matter how hard he tried to understand her reasoning, Lilly was a weak parent, allowing Astrid the freedom to dress like a ghoul, speak like a brat and get her own way.

In order to keep them both alive, he would have to insist that Lilly follow his parenting rules from now on. No exceptions.

TWO

"No way," Astrid said, removing her neatly folded clothes from the suitcase and placing them back in the drawer. "I'm not going anywhere."

Lilly sat on her daughter's bed. Despite Astrid's insistence on being grown-up and independent, her bed was filled with her childhood teddies. Lilly picked up a white fluffy bear, Astrid's favorite stuffed toy. She had always called him, simply, White Bear.

"I'm not asking you to do this, I'm *telling* you," Lilly said, still stinging from Agent McQueen's criticism that Astrid didn't respect her authority. That just wasn't true, at least not all the time. "You don't have a choice."

"Mom, this is crazy. People only go into witness protection programs in the movies. We live in boring Oakmont, remember?"

Lilly wondered how Astrid could have forgotten her terrifying ordeal so quickly. That morning's school run was anything but boring.

"Somebody tried to hurt us today," she said. "I mean *really* hurt us. And you have to admit you were scared."

Astrid swallowed and Lilly saw the fear momentarily

return. "Yeah, I was scared, but we're okay now, and the guy was probably high on drugs or something."

"I already explained this to you, honey," Lilly said. "He deliberately targeted me because of something bad that happened at the bank, and he'll come back. We need to leave town until he's caught, and then we'll be able to come home."

"How long will it take?"

"I don't know, but we should take enough clothes for a week."

"A week? Seriously? It's Kaitlyn's sixteenth birthday party on Saturday night. I can't miss that. And what about school?"

Lilly stroked the soft fur on White Bear. "I know this is hard, but we have to make sacrifices. Our safety is more important than a birthday party or missing a week of school."

Astrid flopped on the bed next to her mother. "Are you sure that this FBI guy isn't exaggerating? He seems kinda repressed, like he's full of trapped gas or something."

Lilly couldn't help but laugh at this fitting description of Agent David McQueen. It was then that she noticed him standing at the slightly open door, listening to their conversation, his head cocked to the side as if amused. Or annoyed. When her gaze met his, he held it for a few seconds, saying nothing.

She tried to imagine this buttoned-up man parenting two daughters, but couldn't envisage him playing with toys or reading books, especially while wearing his dark suit and tie. Given that his children were now adults, she guessed that his age would be somewhere in the midforties, a good ten years her senior, yet he could pass for a much younger man. With a full head of curly brown hair, smooth tanned skin and a neatly trimmed beard, he was attractive without being too polished or high-maintenance. He had an outdoorsy look that was most definitely Lilly's type. Not that it mattered anyway—romance was a thing of the past for her, and her sole focus was placed on raising her daughter.

"May I come into your room, Astrid?" David asked, knocking on the door. "I promise to keep my trapped gas where it is."

Astrid sat upright and shifted closer to Lilly. She clearly wasn't comfortable with the burly FBI agent who had invaded her home.

"Sure," she said, with affected nonchalance. "Whatever."

He entered the room, surveying the mixture of teenage music posters and babyhood relics. He also couldn't fail to notice the colossal mess on the floor. Shoes, purses, belts and makeup palettes were strewn across the carpet, and his expression didn't hide his disapproval.

"I wanted to let you know that we've managed to secure a safe house for the coming week," he said. "Goldie and I will escort you there and remain with you until Gilbert Henderson is in custody."

"Do you have any leads on him?" Lilly asked, desperately hoping that he might have been captured already by a patrol unit.

"We found the stolen van abandoned in a Pittsburgh parking lot, and we've got detectives reviewing the security footage of the stores in the area to see if we can track his movements. He'll crop up on the radar sooner or later, I'm sure of it."

Remembering David's description of this guy as both cunning and smart, Lilly wasn't so sure.

"Why can't we stay here?" Astrid said, picking at chipped nail polish. "You could stay here too and then when this guy comes back, you arrest him." She put her palms up in the air. "Mission complete."

"It's not that easy," David replied. "This house has too many points of entry and it's a single-story home, surrounded by lots of dark hiding places. I'm not comfortable protecting you here." He checked his watch. "I'd like to be gone in one hour. Do you think you could have a suitcase ready by then?"

"So that's it?" Astrid said, rising to stand and fold her arms. "You get to make all the decisions about where and when we go?"

"Yes."

Astrid looked at Lilly imploringly. "Mom," she whined. "I don't want to go."

"You have two options," David said. "You come with me or you place yourself in serious danger. Do you really want to do that?"

Lilly stood between David and Astrid. "That's enough talk of danger," she said, rebuking the FBI agent. "Astrid and I will be ready in an hour." She fixed him with a hard stare. "Okay?"

"There's just one more thing," he said. "We'll be trying to blend in, to look as normal as possible. We don't want to attract any attention when we go outside."

Lilly wasn't sure what he was getting at. "And?"

"And Astrid sticks out like a sore thumb in that gloomy costume she's wearing. She needs to change clothes and wear something more suitable. Might I suggest jeans and a sweatshirt?"

"Gloomy costume?" Astrid said with incredulity. "You're so old and stupid. You don't know anything about being cool."

"Astrid!" Lilly said sharply. "That's enough."

David smiled. "I admit that I don't know anything about being cool, but I know a lot about witness protection, and you cannot wear those type of clothes if you want to fade into the crowd."

"I expect you want me to wear a pretty dress with flowers and bows, right?" Astrid said sarcastically. "Like your own daughters probably did."

Lilly saw a sudden change come over him, a sadness clouding his eyes, and she knew that Astrid had hit a raw nerve.

"This is getting a little out of hand," she said, taking hold of David's arm and leading him to the door. "Astrid, please pack your suitcase and change clothes. You can wear black jeans and your hooded sweatshirt."

"And black lipstick?" Astrid said hopefully.

"Yes, black lipstick too," Lilly replied, feeling too drained to argue on this small point. "Be ready in an hour."

With that, she steered David out of the room and clicked the door closed behind her, instantly hearing rock music playing on Astrid's speaker.

"You shouldn't give in to her like that," David said. "She needs to follow strict instructions."

"Oh, come on," Lilly shot back, her mood darkening. "Do you really think that a little black lipstick is going to attract a huge amount of attention?"

"It's not just the lipstick. It's a slippery slope. Once you give in to one small demand, it soon snowballs into much bigger things. And if you lose control of her, it'll be impossible to get it back."

Lilly breathed slowly in though her nose and out through her mouth. "I know you have an important job to do, and it's understandable that you want Astrid to play by the rules, but she's just a kid. You can't poke fun at her clothes like that and expect her to respect you. She has thoughts and feelings just like you, so quit being so hard on her, okay?"

He seemed to think long and hard about Lilly's reprimand. "I'm sorry, but I'm only saying these things for your own benefit. I don't want you to make the same mistake as I did."

"What mistake?"

He briefly closed his eyes. "It's nothing." He turned to walk down the hallway. "I'll wait in the living room while you pack a suitcase."

Lilly watched him stride away and pondered the words that he had left unsaid.

David kept a close eye on the street outside while Lilly brushed her daughter's hair in the hallway and tied it up in a ponytail. With her bright blond strands and olive-toned skin, Astrid really was a carbon copy of her mother. Both tall and rangy, they possessed a Viking quality, women who were undoubtedly a force to be reckoned with. Lilly was clearly strong-minded and raising a strong-minded daughter, but she had so much to learn about teens. Astrid was already pushing her boundaries, perhaps even going off the rails, and Lilly's response was to compromise. One thing you should never do with an errant teenager is compromise.

Goldie was performing one last security check of the

house, ensuring that the sensor alarms were working correctly. These sensors would give them a warning of unauthorized entry. If Henderson came looking for Lilly and Astrid here, the silent alarm would trigger an immediate police response.

His cell phone buzzed, and he slipped it from his pocket to look at the display, smiling on seeing Chloe's name.

"Hi," he said, hitting the answer button. "How are things in Penn Hills today?"

"Good." She sounded happy, and he was pleased. "The sun is shining."

"Listen, Chloe, I'm glad you called because I have to go away for a week with work, so I won't be able to come see you for a while, okay?"

"Sure, Dad. I'm fine with that. I don't need to see you every day, you know. I'm a grown woman now."

"I know." He found it impossible to cut Chloe's apron strings. "Thanks for reminding me."

"I wanted to tell you that I had a job interview early this morning, and it went really well. I think I'll get it."

"A job interview? Really? Why didn't you tell me? Where is it?"

"Whoa," she said. "One question at a time, Dad."

He deliberately slowed down, remembering that Chloe needed time to process information.

"Okay," he said. "What job is it?"

"An assistant at the local grocery store," she said, with an obvious smile. "It's a nice place and the staff are friendly and the manager said I could take extra time to learn the shelf-stocking system if I need to."

"That's great, honey, really great," he said, feeling disappointment sink deep down into his belly. "I'm proud of you."

Before the accident, Chloe had been expected to graduate top of her class, and the medical profession was her passion. At the age of twenty-one, she should have been a doctor in training, not hoping to stock shelves at a grocery store.

"If I manage to hold down this job, then I might be allowed to move out of my assisted living apartment and rent a regular place with my friends. That would be really cool, right?"

"Yes, it would," he said. "I'll say a prayer for you tonight."

"Thanks, Dad. I'll call back soon. I love you."

"Love you too, sweetie."

He hung up the phone, his stomach a twist of knots. He should have been pleased that Chloe was on the cusp of regaining full independence, preparing to move out of the apartment where a qualified nurse was on hand in case she needed it. Her rehabilitation had been arduous, but she'd made good progress and had regained full use of her body. Yet her brain could only recover up to a point and had lost its ability to think quickly, to retain information and to learn complex things. It pained David to accept that he should carry the burden of blame. If only he hadn't allowed her to go out with her boyfriend that night. If only he'd realized that she was making bad choices. If only he hadn't given her the benefit of the doubt. The words *if only* tormented him.

"Hey." Lilly was standing next to him, wearing a pastel blue sweat suit that was almost the same color as her eyes. "Are you all right? You're miles away."

"Yeah, I'm fine." He pocketed the phone. "Are you guys ready? Goldie is just doing the final checks."

"We're as ready as we'll ever be," Lilly replied, glancing down the hall at Astrid, who was swiping her finger down her phone. "It's crazy to think we'll be prisoners in a strange place for a while. I can't quite get my head around it."

"You won't be prisoners. You'll be in protective custody."

She gave him a thin smile. "It kind of sounds like the same thing to me."

"Not really. Prisoners have a strict routine and they're confined to a small cell for most of the day."

"Okay, okay, I get it. Boy, you really are a stickler, aren't you?"

He raised an eyebrow. "I've been called worse."

She put an index finger on her lips, as if recalling a fact. "I know. I seem to remember somebody calling you old and stupid recently."

He laughed.

"I'm sorry about that," Lilly said. "Astrid sometimes lashes out when she's afraid or unsure. She doesn't mean any harm. Do you think you could cut her some slack?"

"I'll try," he said, knowing that he would struggle to do so. "She can call me as many names as she likes, but you know how I feel about following rules."

"Yes, I do. Even though I only met you a few hours ago, I feel like I understand you perfectly."

He wasn't sure whether this was a good or bad thing. "And how are you holding up, Lilly?"

Moisture collected in her eyes and she took a sharp intake of breath. "I keep thinking about how close I came to death this morning. What would Astrid do without me? Who would look after her? It's terrifying to think about what might happen."

He heard a quiver in her voice and realized that she

was trembling, so he put both hands on her shoulders to comfort her.

"You'll get through this, I promise."

"I don't want Astrid to see me scared," she whispered, leaning into him, wafting a perfume of spiced vanilla. "Can you distract her for a couple minutes while I compose myself?"

He gave one shoulder a squeeze and left her side.

"Hi, Astrid," he said, picking up her suitcase in the hallway. "You look nice."

She rolled her eyes. "I look like a norm."

"A norm?"

"A norm is a normal person. A person like you."

"Oh, right." This was awkward. "Thanks for the compliment."

She tugged at the sweatshirt. "I hate this stuff. I'm just glad that my friends can't see me right now. I mean, who wears sneakers unless they're running?"

At that moment, Astrid reminded him so much of Chloe at the same age, obsessed with her image and the judgment of others. He had tried to placate his daughter at the time, tell her it didn't matter what her friends might think, offer her an alternative viewpoint. He wasn't going down that road again.

"Plenty of people wear sneakers," he said. "That's the whole point. You need to look like everyone else, so I want to see you in sneakers all the time, okay?"

She put one hand on a jutted-out hip. "Don't you ever get tired of being right?"

"Not usually."

Astrid's gaze slid past his, toward the open door of the living room, and landed on her mother.

"Is Mom okay?" she asked. "She looks nervous."

"She's doing fine." Lilly obviously had an astute appreciation of the danger they were facing, whereas Astrid had somehow managed to overlook the fact that a gunman fired a shot at them this morning. "She's just worried about you."

Astrid's expression softened. "Mom worries all the time, about lots of things. She worries about my grades and my confidence and my friends and my future. She never seems to worry about herself."

"That's the life of a parent, Astrid," he said. "Your mother's job is to make sure you're safe and secure all the time. Nobody in the world will ever love you like your parents."

Her softened expression now became hard again, eyes narrowing and lips pinching. "What do you know?" she said, turning her back on him. "You're no expert."

While David stood in bewilderment, wondering what on earth he'd said to provoke such a reaction, Goldie came in through the front door and closed it behind her.

"I've scoped out the street and the car," she said. "It's all clear."

She then clearly noticed Astrid leaning against the wall, stone-faced and silent, arms wrapped round her waist. The older woman immediately enveloped the teenager in a hug and whispered some words of comfort, assuming she was anxious about the risky situation. Goldie was a tough cookie on the outside but loving and warm inside, a trait that had come in handy numerous times when dealing with nervous clients, and David was thankful for it now.

While Astrid was being soothed by Goldie, he approached Lilly.

"I think I upset Astrid," he said. "I'm sorry. I'm not what sure what I said, but Goldie's with her now so she's doing fine."

"Did you mention her father?"

"Ah." Now it became clearer. "Not exactly, but I might have implied that *both* her parents love her."

Lilly lightly brushed his arm. "It's not your fault. It's a touchy subject. Astrid's father hasn't seen her in over two years and it upsets her that he doesn't even try to make contact. She blames me for it. I wish I could make Rylan see what a beautiful daughter he has, but he never seems to listen."

David shook his head. How could a father sleep at night without checking that his little girl was secure and safe? How could a man be so weak and selfish? He felt a new level of respect for Lilly for stepping up and attempting to provide the stability that her daughter badly needed.

"It's tough being a single parent, huh?" he said.

She rubbed her temples over the silky blond strands. "The toughest job in the world. Are you speaking from experience?"

"My wife, Carla, died fifteen years ago, when our daughters were only six and ten years old. I raised them alone."

"I'm so sorry," Lilly said with sincerity. "That must've been hard on all of you."

"It was," he said, reminded of the dark days that had followed the loss of his wife, of the constant fear that he would not be able to fill a mother's shoes. "It's not easy being both mom and dad. There's nobody to pass the baton to when you're at the end of your rope."

"I hear you."

He dropped his voice. "Teenagers can be especially rebellious, and that's when being a single parent really tests your character. You have to stand firm and be the boss."

"Is that what you did?"

"That's what I should've done." The regrets never stopped tumbling through his mind. "And I just wanted to give you the benefit of my parenting experience."

"Thank you," she said, skirting past him. "I'll bear it in mind."

But he knew she wouldn't. As she went to her daughter and hugged her tenderly, he saw that she was a parent who would struggle to implement the tough love approach. Astrid could pout and cry and get away with doing whatever she wanted, even if it meant going to a party with her drunk and reckless boyfriend. Just one small decision could wreak untold consequences.

And Lilly had no idea of the terrible choices that a teenage mind could make.

"We're leaving now," Lilly said, removing one of her daughter's earbuds. "You need to turn off your music and keep your wits about you."

David held out his hand. "And I have to confiscate your cell phone until further notice. I want all devices which emit a signal."

"What?" Astrid's mouth dropped open as she turned to Lilly. "Really?"

"No arguments, Astrid," Lilly said, slipping the cell from her daughter's jeans pocket, unplugging the earphones and handing it to the agent. She then unzipped Astrid's backpack and took out her iPad. "You can have them back later."

David took both devices in his hands. "I never said that."

"But it's important to her," Lilly protested. "Teenagers live their whole lives on social media, you must know that."

"Phone signals are easy to track, even when they're not connected to the internet. If Astrid wants to log into Smartchat, she can use one of our specially encrypted devices."

Astrid burst out laughing. "What is Smartchat? Is that like Snapchat for old people?"

He ignored the ridicule. "I'd rather you didn't log into any online accounts for the next few days, but if you really feel that it's necessary, then you can look but not interact."

"I can't post anything?"

"Certainly not. No comments, no messages and absolutely no selfies." He put the phone and iPad into a drawer of the hallway dresser. "We'll leave these here until you get back."

"How will I keep in touch with Noah?"

"You can't," David said. "I need a promise from you that you'll contact nobody while we're in the safe house. You're under my rules now."

Lilly began to bristle with irritation. Astrid was *her* daughter and *her* responsibility, and David should have let *her* relay all this information, rather than lay down the law himself. It was very clear that this FBI agent didn't rate her parenting skills very highly, and she found herself feeling undermined by his intrusive behavior.

"Make the promise, Astrid," she said, trying to wrest back control. "It's only for a little while."

Astrid groaned. "I promise."

"Okay," David said. "Let's go."

Lilly noticed her daughter's face become ashen as they approached the open front door, where Goldie stood, waiting to escort them to the car.

"We'll be okay, won't we, Mom?" Astrid asked. "This

crazy guy wouldn't be stupid enough to try and hurt us while we've got two bodyguards, would he?"

Lilly wasn't sure whether to tell the truth—that she simply had no idea—but she decided that a small lie was the best approach.

"He wouldn't be that stupid, honey," she said, putting an arm around Astrid. "We're in the hands of trained experts here."

"You're clear to get in the car," Goldie said, as they stepped out into the cool and breezy afternoon. "Both in the back seat, please."

The day had now taken on a new hue, one of danger and malice. The scenery beyond Lilly's home was exactly the same as before, but the neat suburban houses and leafy trees now hid something sinister and strange. This world no longer felt like hers. It was alien somehow, and she wasn't enjoying the sensation. Somebody had invaded her haven of peace and contentment.

Goldie opened the back door of the black SUV in the driveway and Astrid climbed inside, murmuring appreciatively at the plush upholstery and gadget-laden dash. They were unused to luxury in their daily lives.

"Lilly, Lilly, wait up." She looked up sharply to see Mr. Peters hurrying around the fence that divided their front yards. He was carrying a brown box, saying, "I have something for you."

Goldie and David immediately switched to high alert, placing their hands on their weapons and scanning the area.

David rushed to her side. "Who is this man?"

"It's my neighbor, John Peters. I've known him for thirteen years."

David quickly pulled out his badge and held it out

front, keeping Mr. Peters at arm's length. "Sir, can I ask you to remain where you are and state your business?"

Mr. Peters appeared puzzled to be met with such a command. "Um… I have a package for Lilly." He peered at the badge. "Are you from the FBI?"

"Put the package on the ground," David ordered, pocketing the badge and drawing his gun but keeping the barrel pointed down.

Mr. Peters obviously wasn't sure how to react. "I didn't do anything wrong," he said. "The delivery guy said he couldn't get an answer from Lilly's house so I signed for the package on her behalf." He looked between Lilly and David. "That's okay, isn't it?"

"I told you to put the package on the ground," David repeated, louder this time. "Now."

Mr. Peters reacted in an instant, placing the box on the ground as if it were suddenly red-hot.

"Now step away from it," David said. "Where did the delivery guy go after you signed for this package? Did he have a vehicle?"

"I didn't check, but he was wearing a uniform and he had a clipboard. He looked very official."

"Where did he go?"

"I don't know. I'm sorry but I didn't think to take notice." By now Mr. Peters appeared genuinely afraid, concerned that he might have inadvertently done something wrong. "The label on the box says it contains drapes and cushions."

David glanced at Lilly. "Did you order home furnishings?"

She racked her brain to recall any recent online purchases. "I don't think so."

"Get Astrid out of the car." David said, before turning to Goldie. "We need to get them back in the house and call the bomb squad."

Fear flooded Lilly's body. "You think it's a bomb?"

"We have to take every precaution," he replied. "It might be nothing, but let's be cautious."

Astrid slid from the car and stared at the cardboard box on the driveway, its beige, boring exterior seemingly innocuous.

"It's just a package," she said, walking toward it. "Why are you guys so worked up about a cardboard box?"

"No, Astrid," David called. "Stay away from it and go back inside."

Lilly grabbed hold of Astrid's sleeve. "Come on, honey, let's do what he says."

Astrid shook her head in disbelief. "I can't believe you're all terrified of some drapes and cushions. Mom probably ordered them and forgot."

But then the box began to beep, slow at first but quickly building, like an alarm clock working its way up to a crescendo.

"Go, Go, Go!" David yelled, pushing Lilly and Astrid toward the house. "Everybody clear the area."

Lilly clutched Astrid's hand and ran to her front door, stumbling over the threshold and falling into the hallway. She just managed to pull her daughter into an embrace when a flash of light burned her eyes. The sound of the explosion came a split second later.

And then there was silence.

THREE

Lilly lay on the floor in her hallway, clutching Astrid as tightly as she could. The overpowering smell and taste of smoke was stinging her throat and she made a futile attempt to waft the fumes from Astrid's mouth.

"David," she called. "Where are you?"

"I'm here," he said, his dark silhouette filling the open door. He came to kneel next to her, his hair tousled and his skin grimy but apparently otherwise unscathed. "Are either of you injured?"

Lilly held her daughter's face in her hands. "You're okay, aren't you, honey?"

Astrid nodded. "It really was a bomb," she said shakily. "He was right."

"It was instinct," David said. "You learn to be wary of everything in this job."

He pulled his radio from the clip on his waist and spoke quickly and clearly into it, requesting the police and an ambulance. All the while, he kept a firm hand on Lilly's arm, pressing her down to the floor.

"Who's the ambulance for?" she asked. "Is Goldie hurt?"

"She's fine," he replied. "We managed to shield ourselves behind the car, but Mr. Peters took some shrapnel to the leg. It was a crude homemade bomb, packed with shards of metal, designed to inflict maximum damage. His injury isn't life-threatening, and Goldie's tending to his wounds now. I need the two of you to go into a locked room until backup arrives. There's a chance that Henderson is watching the house."

Lilly thought hard, struggling to focus. "The only room with a lock is the bathroom."

David lifted her to her feet. "Go there, lock the door and wait for me." He took his gun from its holster and handed it to her. "Do you know how to use it?"

"Yes."

Having grown up with a father who loved hunting, Lilly was experienced in handling all types of weapons, but since Astrid's birth, she'd decided against keeping one in the house. Taking care of a child involved making tough decisions, and she took each one seriously, weighing the risks before choosing the option that was the most nurturing.

"Shoot if you need to," David said, helping Astrid to stand. "I'll be back in just a few minutes."

David strode through the front door beyond which Lilly saw a plume of thick black smoke rising from behind the car. The windshield of the SUV was shattered, embedded with many silver fragments from the bomb, creating an almost beautiful spiderweb design.

"We gotta get into the bathroom, Mom," Astrid said, heading down the hallway. "We should do what he says."

Lilly followed, pleased by her daughter's sudden conversion to following David's rules. When they had both entered the bathroom, she slipped the lock into place and pulled the wooden cabinet across the door. It wouldn't offer much in the way of resistance, but anything was better than nothing.

"Okay," she said, placing the gun in the sink and checking that the small window was securely fastened. "I think that's all we can do for now."

Astrid had slid to the floor and was sitting on the striped shower mat, her knees pulled up to her chest. Lilly dropped to her level and drew her into an embrace.

"I know this is scary," she said. "But we're in safe hands. Everything will be fine."

"You don't know that for sure," Astrid mumbled into her mom's sweater. "They're just empty words."

"David and Goldie are trained FBI agents and they know what they're doing."

Astrid pushed Lilly away to pull a tissue from her jeans pocket. Rather than use it, she crumpled it inside a clenched fist. "They couldn't stop the bomb though. It blew up right outside our door."

"David prevented you from going near it, didn't he? He kept you safe."

"But what about the next time, or the time after that?" Astrid was working herself into a highly anxious state. "He can't stop every single danger. He's not a superhero."

Lilly lightly held Astrid's chin between her thumb and forefinger, the way she used to when Astrid was a toddler. "We're also being protected by someone who *is* like a superhero."

"Oh, come on, Mom, not this God stuff again. The Bible is just a fairy story, like *Lord of the Rings*."

Lilly's heart was still hammering in the aftermath of the explosion and she took a moment to try to calm it before speaking.

Placing a hand over her chest, she said, "God is way better than Gandalf."

Astrid laughed and Lilly was pleased to feel some tension lift.

"Are you sure about that?" Astrid said with a smile. "Because Gandalf is awesome."

"I can promise you that God is stronger than a billion Gandalfs," Lilly said, remembering how Astrid adored *The Lord of the Rings* books when she was in middle school and insisted on having them read to her every night. "He's stronger than you can ever imagine."

Astrid's smile faded. "I hope you're right, because we need somebody special to help us now. I'm frightened, Mom. I want everything to go back to how it used to be."

"It will, sweetheart," Lilly said, stroking her daughter's creamy unblemished cheek. "I give you my word."

But in an instant, the mood changed. Astrid jumped to her feet, screaming and pointing at the window, where the outline of a head could be seen peering through the frosted glass. Lilly grabbed for the gun and aimed it toward the danger.

"Who's there?" she called. "I'm armed."

"It's Noah," a voice called back. "I'm looking for Astrid."

Lilly lowered her weapon and leaned against the wall, breathing a sigh of relief. Noah was Astrid's boyfriend, a sweet kid from two blocks away who doted on her and showered her with compliments. She reached up and opened the window, seeing Noah's mop of curly hair come into view.

"You need to leave," Lilly said. "You might have noticed that there's a serious situation going on here. It's dangerous."

Noah craned his head to peer round Lilly and catch

sight of Astrid. "I was worried when you called to say you were sick, so I skipped lunch to come check on you."

Astrid walked to the window and put her fingers on the ledge to stand on tiptoe. "I'm okay, but I have to leave town for a few days and I'm not sure when I'll be coming back, so you'll have to get used to life without me for a while. I'm not allowed to contact you. The bossy FBI guy took my cell phone."

"Lunchtime is almost over, Noah," Lilly said, pulling Astrid away from the window. "Leave via the backyard and head straight back to school. Promise me you'll do that."

Before Noah could reply, the bathroom door flew open and the cabinet was flung across the room, hitting the wall and spilling its contents. David stood in the hallway, gun raised, his features fixed in concentration. Noah instinctively ducked down below the window, shouting, "Don't shoot."

"Who's this?" David said. "I heard a scream."

Lilly's words came out in a rush, trying to relay as much information as possible, "It's Noah. He's not a threat. He's just a kid."

The sound of numerous sirens could be heard heading their way and David holstered his weapon, narrowing his eyes at the skinny boy who was rising from his hiding place, deep dimples on his cheeks created by his sheepish smile.

"What are you doing here?" David asked harshly. "Why aren't you at school?"

"I came to check on Astrid because she's sick," he said, his brown eyes darting around the room awkwardly under the scrutiny of undeniable authority. "I'm sorry. I didn't know what was going on." He scratched his head. "What *is* going on?"

"Astrid and her mom are in a dangerous situation at the moment and they need to go away for a while," David said. "We'd hoped to keep it under wraps but it looks like that's now impossible." When Noah opened his mouth to speak, David reached up to the window handle. "Don't ask any questions. Go back to school and Astrid will contact you when it's safe, but that might not be for quite a while."

Noah leaned his head to shout through the narrowing gap of the closing window, "I love you, Astrid."

David turned to Lilly with a frown. "Is he Astrid's boyfriend?"

"Yes."

"You let her have a boyfriend?"

Lilly placed the gun back in the sink, comforted by the sirens that had screeched to a halt outside her home. There was now a heavy police presence in the vicinity and Henderson would surely be long gone.

"Astrid is almost sixteen years old," she said. "She's old enough to make these types of decisions for herself."

"You said earlier that she's still a child."

"Yes, technically she still is a child," Lilly said, suppressing her annoyance. "She's at that difficult in-between age, where she's not yet an adult but deserving of a little freedom."

David's eyebrows shot up so comically high that Lilly almost laughed in spite of the situation.

"Astrid's not yet wise enough to know which boys have decent morals," he said. "I'd strongly advise you to reconsider allowing her to have a boyfriend."

"I've known Noah since he was tiny," Lilly said, thinking back to his baby curls and cute dimples. "His mom is an old friend and his family are good people. Noah and Astrid have a really sweet and innocent relationship, and he would never hurt her. Ever."

"You can't be sure of that."

"Well," Lilly said, folding her arms. "Of course, I could wrap Astrid in cotton balls and keep her locked away in a closet until she's twenty-one. Or I could live in the real world and take a chance that everything will work out okay in the end."

"Now you're mocking me."

She ran her fingers through her hair. "I don't mean to be unkind, but you're a little intense, and you're making judgments based on assumptions. Astrid is rude sometimes, but she isn't as immature as you think."

"She's fifteen. She is the dictionary definition of immature."

Astrid coughed. "I'm right here, you know," she said with a small wave. "I can hear every word you're saying."

Lilly suddenly realized how inappropriate it was to discuss Astrid's character and failings in front of her. It was wrong, yet it pained her to admit that she was actually enjoying this interaction with David. Yes, he was stubborn and maddening but he was taking an interest in Astrid, showing concern for her well-being and being more of a father than Rylan had ever been. Lilly felt herself drawn to him because of it, and a flicker of attraction somehow sparked into life. Here was somebody with whom she could really, truly talk about the difficulties of raising Astrid. It was just a shame they weren't on the same page.

Astrid came to stand between them. "It's weird to

hear you guys arguing about me when a bomb just exploded outside our house and Mr. Peters is bleeding on the driveway." She shrugged. "And I thought *I* was meant to be the immature one."

Lilly and David stared at each other, both shamefaced by this timely rebuke from a teenager.

"I'm sorry, honey," Lilly said, holding David's gaze. "We're both sorry."

David put a hand on Astrid's arm. Lilly guessed that the gesture was meant to be comforting and reassuring but it came off as awkward.

"You remind me of my youngest daughter," he said a little stiffly. "And that makes me overprotective. I'm sorry if I upset you."

Astrid looked up at him. "What's your daughter's name?"

"Chloe."

"Well, it must be a great feeling for Chloe to have a dad who cares about her as much as you do. I wish..."

Astrid stopped mid-sentence and dropped her head, suddenly dejected. Lilly assumed that she was about to mention her own father and his lack of care for her.

"I understand, honey," Lilly said softly. "Let's go check on Mr. Peters and I'll call the principal to make sure that Noah makes it back to school."

"Stay close to me," David said, picking up the gun from the sink and placing it in a chest holster. "Don't leave my sight, not even for a second."

Lilly took a deep breath and nodded. If the last few hours were anything to go by, the next few days would be full of disagreement regarding the discipline and management of Astrid. But she and David would just have to learn to put their differences aside and cooperate for the sake of everyone's safety.

Astrid's life might depend on their ability to work as a team.

David passed a cup of hot tea to Lilly. "It's sweet," he said. "I thought you might need it after the shock of this morning."

She took the tea and held the cup in her hands, wrapping her fingers around the china as if to warm them. The four-bedroomed apartment that had been designated as their safe house was incredibly cold, most likely left unheated for months. After switching on the thermostat, Goldie was walking through the place, ensuring that each radiator was working at full capacity. She often liked to joke to David that she was the handyman of their professional partnership, and her toolbox was always in the trunk of the car, ready for any necessary repairs or tinkering.

"I can't believe that I was on my way to work a few hours ago, thinking about what to cook for dinner, worrying that I would be late for work, stressing about Astrid's birthday party." Lilly took a sip of the tea. "The normal, mundane kind of stuff that seemed so important this morning."

David settled himself on the sofa next to her, making himself as comfortable as possible in this chilly and unwelcoming apartment with no trace of home comforts, not even a cushion.

"A birthday party, huh?" he said with a smile. "Let me guess—Astrid wants a big celebration with a whole bunch of friends and a lot of bling."

She laughed. "How did you know?"

"Just a hunch. Is she okay? She was quiet in the car."

After waiting a few hours for a replacement vehicle to arrive, the journey to the apartment had taken only thirty minutes. David's original plan was to take Lilly and Astrid farther afield, but the lost time meant that he needed to change his strategy. Instead of driving out of state, he'd requested that the FBI source a property in Pittsburgh, and they'd rented this nondescript apartment in an anonymous block, where nobody would bother them or care to notice their presence. It was ideal. He knew that Henderson had dumped his stolen van in a parking lot just ten miles away, but that added to the appeal of the city. It was surely the last location the con man would consider as their hiding place.

"Astrid's in her bedroom, settling in," Lilly said. "She decided that she wanted the room with the lime-green wallpaper and pink carpet. She thinks it's retro."

He laughed. "I'm old enough to remember when retro was cool the first time around."

"She likes old things," Lilly said. "She doesn't care for mass-produced, generic kind of stuff. She likes to be unique, which is ironic because all her friends think exactly the same way."

"The problem with teenagers is that they mostly don't know what they like."

"I don't disagree on that."

David sipped his tea, consciously trying to keep the conversation on an even keel. He had clearly overstepped in previous discussions and irritated Lilly with his advice and concerns. Lilly obviously didn't know why he felt so strongly about Astrid's behavior, didn't understand what his family had gone through due to Chloe's actions. He decided that he would attempt to tread more carefully.

"Is Astrid hungry?" he asked, eyeing the dark night

between the gap in the drapes. "I'll be getting some takeout soon."

"She's writing in her journal at the moment, but she'll eat pretty much anything."

He was surprised. "Astrid writes a journal?"

"Yeah, since she was ten years old. She bottles up her feelings a lot, so it helps to get them down on paper." Lilly's face took on a melancholic expression. "She can tell her journal things that she doesn't want to tell me."

"Like what?"

"About her dad, mostly. She's spent her whole life being disappointed in him, and I can't make it better for her, so she often thinks I don't care." She closed her eyes, revealing smudged mascara on her lids, and David fought a strange urge to reach over and run his thumb across the black streaks. "I keep wondering if I should tell her father what's happening. I guess he's entitled to know where she is." She fixed her icy blue eyes on him. "What do you think?"

"Does he have shared custody?"

Lilly laughed, high and brittle. "Technically, yes, but realistically, no."

"Legally, he has a right to know that Astrid is temporarily in protective custody, so I think you should call him." As much as David didn't want to give this guy any unearned authority over Astrid, he was her father and must be respected as such. "Tell him that you're both safe, but don't give any details about the case or your location."

"Can I use your phone?"

"Sure." He slid the cell from his pocket and handed it to her. "It's a secure line."

He watched Lilly punch in the number on the keypad, noticing her jawline tense and her brow furrow. She clearly didn't relish this task and he rose from the sofa to walk into the kitchen and give her a little space. As he heard her begin to speak, he felt a sensation descend, an unfamiliar one that caught him off guard. He realized that he was both jealous and angry. This stranger had not only betrayed his daughter but had also hurt Lilly. Lilly was wrong about plenty of things, but she had a good heart, and she deserved a good man. Rylan had once possessed a golden opportunity to be part of a loving family and he had squandered the chance. He was clearly a fool.

"No, Rylan," Lilly was saying, exasperation clear in her voice. "I'm not calling to ask for money. I never ask you for money. This is important. Astrid and I are in FBI protective custody." After a few moments of silence, she seemed to finally lose her patience. "Never mind. It doesn't matter. I thought you should know what's happening but it's clear that you don't really care. I hope you enjoy your vacation. Goodbye."

David returned to the living room to find her sitting on the couch, forearms on her knees, pressing the edge of the cell to her forehead with her eyes squeezed tightly shut.

"Tough call, huh?" he said.

She stood and handed him the phone. "Rylan is on vacation in Florida, and he wasn't very pleased about being bothered while he's at Disney World with his new girlfriend." She let out a moan of frustration. "He's got it in his head that I'm just looking for money or attention. Why did I have to choose such a deadbeat dad for my daughter? Why couldn't I have chosen someone like you?"

David felt his color rise. He hadn't blushed since he was a boy, and he tried to hide it by coughing and staring at his feet.

"I wasn't such a great dad either," he said, pushing his hands into the pockets of his suit pants. "I made plenty of mistakes too."

"All parents make mistakes, but at least you were there for your daughters. You tried your best."

Her words seemed to echo in his mind. Had he tried his best? Could he have done more? How he wished he could turn back time and be stricter in his approach. He would much rather Chloe hate him for being tough than to see her with irreversible brain damage. That's why he couldn't let Lilly drop the ball with Astrid.

"Yeah, I tried my best," he said. "But it wasn't enough. If I could do it all over again, I'd be a different kind of father. I'd do it better."

She frowned at him. "Your daughters are grown women, right?"

"Right."

"And are they happy?"

"Yes."

"Are they kind and decent people?"

He didn't even need to think about that one. "Absolutely."

She smiled. "Then you don't need to do it all over again. You got it right the first time."

He inwardly groaned and raised his gaze to the ceiling. Lilly didn't understand, and he didn't want to explain it to her. Discussing the accident was always painful, always nudging his regrets.

As if sensing his uneasiness, Lilly said, "You're obviously a good father, David. Some men don't deserve to be fathers and Rylan is one of those men. I'm starting to think that Astrid is better off without him."

"Mom!" David snapped his head sideways to see Astrid in the doorway, her blond hair flattened on one side from where she had been lying on a pillow. And her mouth was dropped open in horror and disbelief. "Why would you say I'm better off without Dad? It's not true."

David ran a hand down his face. Of all the conversations for Astrid to overhear, this one might be the worst. Some careful backtracking would be needed.

"Oh, Astrid," Lilly gasped, immediately rushing to her side. "I didn't want you to hear that." She ruffled her daughter's hair, disturbing the flattened strands. "Forget I said it."

"How can I forget it?" Astrid retorted, pushing her mother away. "You said it like you really meant it." She caught David's eye for a split second and he saw a chasm of grief that was quickly covered with rage. "I knew you secretly hated Dad. I knew it all along."

"I don't hate him, honey," Lilly said, her eyes now glassy with moisture. "I'm disappointed in him. It's different."

"Disappointed in him," Astrid repeated, imitating her mother's cool and measured tone. "That's just adult speak for hating on someone."

Lilly maintained her calm demeanor, at least externally. "I just telephoned your father to tell him that we're both in protective custody. I thought he would like to know, but his offhand reaction made me angry and upset, and I spoke harshly without thinking. It's totally my fault and I hope you can forgive me."

Lilly began to wring her index finger in the other hand, as if comforting herself in the face of Astrid's cold and defensive body language, warning her mother to keep a distance. David found it difficult to watch the argument unfold, knowing that it wasn't his place to step in, but feeling his temper rise at the insolence being displayed by Astrid.

"I want to speak to Dad," Astrid said impulsively. "Call him back."

"That's not possible," Lilly said. "He's on vacation and he asked not to be disturbed again."

"I don't believe you."

"It's not a good time to call him right now, but maybe we could send him a text from David's cell and ask when he'd be available for a conversation." Lilly was desperately trying to appease her daughter and David's disapproval grew. "How does that sound?"

"I want to call him," Astrid demanded with a stamp of her foot. "Now."

"I told you he's on vacation."

"You're a liar," Astrid yelled. "And I hate you."

"That's enough," David said, using the kind of deep voice that always made people sit up and take notice. He pointed to the door. "Astrid, go to your room and stay there until you're ready to apologize."

Lilly held her palm in midair. "Actually, David, I think you should stay out of this."

"You need my help here," he said. "That much is obvious."

Astrid adopted a slouchy posture. "You can't tell me what to do. You're not my dad."

"No, I'm not your dad, but I can certainly tell you what to do," he said, continuing to point to the door. "You may have your mom eating out of your hand, but I will not tolerate this level of disrespect. Go to your room." When she failed to move, he added, "Or I can remove the TV from your bedside dresser. It's your choice."

Astrid's shoulders dropped and she let out a high-pitched whine. "I hate you too," she said, storming though the door. "I hate everything here. It sucks."

This insult was water off a duck's back to David. He didn't care whether he had earned a place in Astrid's good books. He cared that he had authority over her.

But Lilly was clearly unhappy with his actions. "Who on earth do you think you are?" she challenged. "Astrid will now go into her shell and be silent for days. She's very sensitive where her father is concerned, and you behaved like a bull in a china shop."

"I did what needed to be done," he said flatly. "She runs rings around you."

"I know it might appear that way," Lilly said. "But I prefer to try and reason with her than be a tyrant."

"Oh, come on, Lilly," he said, feeling oddly as though they were arguing like a married couple. "I'm no tyrant. I'm just instilling a little respect in her. She needs to abide by some rules."

Lilly grabbed a handful of her blond hair and held it in a fist at her scalp, her exasperation clear. "You're driving me crazy, you know that? You have no idea who Astrid is, but you act like you do. I'm her mother and I know her better than anyone else. She's actually wise beyond her years. Underneath all the anger and rudeness, there is a scared little girl, and she needs love and kindness and support."

"Love and kindness and support won't save her from the cruel world out there," he said. "You're kidding yourself if you think you're doing her any favors by treating her with kid gloves."

"If I think kid gloves are necessary, then I'll go right ahead and use them." By now, her eyes were blazing. "I know my daughter."

"I thought I knew my daughter too," he said harshly. "I thought she was mature and smart, but it turns out that I gave her far too much credit. You may think that Astrid is wise but she's not. She's a child, and if you don't start taking a firmer hand in her upbringing, she could end up in a hospital bed being fed through a tube and facing years of grueling rehabilitation just to learn to walk again."

Lilly fell silent, her eyes scanning David's face, confusion evident.

"What are you talking about?" she said gently. "Did something bad happen to your daughter?"

"I said too much already." He mentally reprimanded himself for losing focus. "We need to get ourselves back on track. I'll be drawing up a code of conduct to follow while we're here. I'd appreciate your support in getting Astrid to read it. It's vital that we're all singing from the same song sheet."

"Are you sure you don't want to talk about your daughter?" Lilly said, ignoring his attempt to deflect. "It never helps to internalize your emotions." She tried to smile. "Don't take my word for it—just look at Astrid as an example of what happens when you bottle things up."

Much to his relief, Goldie entered the room, sparing him the embarrassment of disentangling himself from this conversation. He really needed to talk about something else. But unfortunately, Goldie wasn't bringing good news.

"I just got a call from headquarters," she said to David. "Apparently your cell was busy."

"Lilly was using it," he said, noting Goldie's anxious manner as she hovered at the drapes, peering through. "What's going on?"

"Maybe nothing, but we might have to move quickly."

"Why?" They had barely settled in. "What's happened?"

"A few minutes ago, a truck was stolen from a builder's yard a few blocks away," she said, continuing to peek through the window, gun in hand. "The security guard saw the thief drive away and his description matches Henderson perfectly."

"Mr. Berger struck me as a fairly average guy though," Lilly said hopefully. "His description could apply to a lot of other men, right?"

"I take your point, Lilly," Goldie replied. "But the truck is fitted with an antitheft tracker and it's heading our way, which we can't put down to coincidence. We got Pittsburgh police patrols out trying to intercept him, and two officers are sitting in an unmarked car on the street as an extra precaution, but we know that he's smart. If he's discovered our location, he'll find a way to get to us."

"My gut is telling me to get us out of here," David said, pulling out his cell. "We leave right now. I'll make some calls."

"I'll go tell Astrid," Lilly said, heading for the hallway. "We'll be ready in two minutes."

As David dialed the number of his boss in order to request yet another safe house, he racked his brain to consider ways in which he might have inadvertently led Henderson to their location. He thought he'd taken every precaution.

So how had they been compromised so quickly?

FOUR

"We have to go, honey," Lilly said, picking up her daughter's belongings from the floor and shoving them roughly into her suitcase. "David has found a new safe house for us."

Astrid was lying on the bed silently, facedown, her head buried in the floral duvet.

"I know you're upset, and I promise that we can talk about your father later," Lilly said. "Right now we need to focus on what's important, and that's staying out of danger."

Astrid rolled over and sat up, holding White Bear in her hands. "Are we in danger?" Her eyes were red and puffy. "Is that why we have to leave?"

Lilly sank to her knees and peered under the bed, leaning beneath the mattress to retrieve a dropped tissue. David had given strict instructions to leave literally nothing behind.

"We might have been found." She didn't want to strike too much fear into Astrid, but she needed to impart a sense of urgency. "It might be nothing, but David wants to be cautious."

"Oh, really?" Astrid's tone was mocking. "It's not like David to be cautious. He's normally such a free spirit."

"That's quite enough sarcasm," Lilly said, rising to stand too quickly and seeing stars. She sat on the bed to let the dizziness pass and reached out to touch her daughter's ankle. "Please don't be difficult, Astrid. David already thinks I'm too soft on you, and I want to show him that you respect my authority."

"Why do you care what he thinks?"

Lilly stood and placed the last of Astrid's belongings into her case. "I don't know why I care what he thinks, but I do."

Astrid jumped from the bed. "Oh, no, Mom, please don't tell me you like this guy."

"No, of course I don't." She took White Bear from Astrid's hand and placed him on top of the clothes before zipping the case closed. "I just want him to see that I'm a strong, capable mother."

"So you want *him* to like *you*?"

"No. Yes. Not in a romantic way." Lilly opened the door, wheeling the case alongside her. "Let's leave that particular conversation in this room, shall we?"

Astrid pushed her feet into her sneakers. "I'm starving. When do we eat?"

"We'll ask Goldie to stop on the way to the new safe house and get some takeout. Come on. Let's hustle."

"Okay, okay."

Astrid strutted past her mother into the hallway, where Goldie was crawling along the carpet, knocking on the skirting board and pulling at it with her fingertips, seemingly probing for cavities behind it. She looked up as mother and daughter appeared in her line of sight and quickly put a finger to her lips, motioning for them to be silent. Then she pulled a notepad from her pocket and wrote on the top sheet, *Signal detected. Searching for bugs. Say nothing.*

Lilly and Astrid locked both eyes and hands.

"Mom," Astrid whispered. "Can electronic bugs hurt you?"

She leaned in close to whisper back, "No, they can't hurt you. They're just listening devices."

Lilly led Astrid by the hand into the living room where David was holding what looked like a small radio, sweeping it across the walls and carpet, over the coffee table and couch. When he saw them approach, he pointed to the front door, mouthing the words, *Wait there.* Lilly's suitcase was already sitting in the hallway, having never even been unpacked, but the contents of her purse had been spilled out onto the carpet next to it. She and Astrid gathered up her notebook, makeup palettes and eyeglasses to place them back into the leather purse. Lilly fastened the clasp with shaking fingers and Astrid put both hands around her mom's and squeezed tight.

Lilly looked up and smiled appreciatively. Despite displaying remarkable immaturity and rudeness at times, Astrid knew precisely when to show kindness and compassion. She was just learning how to be an adult, and even though her progress was slow, it was constant. Hopefully, David would understand this soon enough.

"Just one more place to check," he said, suddenly looming over them, running his device across Astrid's suitcase. "All clear. Goldie picked up a transmission signal for a brief moment, but it seems to have vanished. Maybe it came from next door. I apologize for emptying your purse, Lilly, but I wanted to be thorough."

"What's going on?" Lilly said, accepting his hand to help her up. "What are you hoping to find?"

"Eavesdropping bugs or GPS signals," he said. "If I'm right about Henderson having found us, we have to face the possibility that someone on the inside is assisting him."

Lilly gripped his hand firmly. "Seriously?"

"I'd like to think it's unlikely we have a mole in the FBI," David replied. "But let's keep an open mind."

He put a hand on Astrid's shoulder but she shrank under his touch. "You okay, Astrid? I'm sorry we had a fight earlier. I hope we can forget about it and move on."

She shrugged his hand off her shoulder. "Whatever."

"You look a little pale."

"She's hungry," Lilly interjected. "She needs to eat."

Astrid had a different explanation. "I'm a goth, Mom. We're always pale."

Lilly smiled. "Of course. I forgot."

Behind David, she saw Goldie walking through the living room, eyes roving across every square inch, her red curls cascading over her face as she darted her head back and forth.

"Listen up, guys," Goldie said, striding toward them, rubbing her hands together. "Let's remember to stay quiet, stick together, remain calm and look out for each other. If you spot anything unusual or suspicious, don't shout or scream. Stop where you are and hold up your hand like this." She raised her right hand. "And David and I will step into action. Okay?"

Lilly found herself liking David's partner more and more. Goldie was strong and confident, the kind of woman she hoped Astrid might become. Astrid also clearly admired the FBI agent, because she went to stand close to her, almost using Goldie as a shield.

"Can I ask you something?" Astrid said quietly.

Goldie smiled. "Sure."

"If Henderson has found us, won't he be waiting for us to leave? We might be walking into a trap."

"That's a very smart question, Astrid," Goldie replied. "You might make a good agent one day, because you're clearly thinking ahead. We already considered this possibility, which is why we have two police officers right outside the front of the building and another two stationed in the underground parking lot. If Henderson is here, he'll have to get through four armed officers, so I think we'll be safe." She winked. "And then he'd have to get through me and I'm the toughest of all."

David laughed. "It's true. Goldie used to be in the Army, so she really knows her stuff. She'll lead the way, you and your mom will walk behind her and I'll guard the rear. We'll get you two safely in the car and I'll briefly return for the suitcases. Are we all clear on that?"

The three women nodded their affirmation and Goldie opened the door, checking the interior hallway both ways before leading them out into the dingy quietness.

"We'll be fine, honey," Lilly said as they passed door after door in the hall, all identical white wood with red numbers in the center. "Don't worry."

"It's so quiet," Astrid whispered. "Where is everybody?"

"A lot of these apartments are empty," David said from behind. "The newer and more luxurious complexes in the city have enticed people away from these old blocks."

"I don't like it. It's spooky."

David felt his shoes sticking slightly to the dirty carpet. "I think that's something we can finally agree on,

Astrid. This place has gotten much worse since the last time we were here."

Up ahead, Goldie stopped at the elevator and waited. Behind a nearby door, there was a clunk and a thud. A man let out a curse word and another man's voice rose in anger. A muffled argument ensued. Lilly didn't like the vibes and she drew Astrid close, putting an arm around her waist.

"Let's use the stairs, Goldie," David said. "I don't trust the elevator."

"Sure thing." Goldie opened the door to the stairwell, which was as poorly lit as the hallway. "Next time I come back here, I'm bringing a ton of one-hundred-watt lightbulbs," she said, holding the door open for Lilly and Astrid to walk through. "This low lighting makes me uneasy."

Stepping into the concrete stairwell, Lilly shivered against the cold. There was a strong smell of ammonia, graffiti on the walls, and the bulb above her head was flickering, creating a strobe effect that was straight out of a horror movie. The low hum of the electricity only added to her fear and the thought of a criminal mastermind being around every corner was almost too much to bear. Astrid didn't deserve to be caught up in this.

David must have sensed her anxiety because he came to stand close behind her, rubbing her shoulders quickly to warm her.

"I'm right here, okay?" he said gently. "I won't leave your side. I promise."

Lilly took hold of Astrid's hand and began to follow Goldie down the stairs, her sneakered feet occasionally squeaking on the smooth and glossy concrete. Despite her reservations about David, his reassurance was both timely and comforting. She had needed to hear those words, to be reminded that someone strong and protective was watching out for them. Rylan had never shown this kind of care or concern for her, not even when she was pregnant, and it made her a little sad to realize what she had missed.

Goldie moved swiftly and silently down several flights of stairs, as fluid and graceful as a cat, one hand resting on her holstered weapon beneath her suit jacket. Just as they reached the underground parking lot, she stopped in her tracks, held up her right hand and froze. Astrid almost fell over her own feet, struggling to stop just as quickly, and Lilly grabbed her arm, pulling her upright.

Nobody spoke.

"I thought I heard something," Goldie whispered. "Did anyone else hear anything?"

Lilly and David answered, "No," in unison, but Astrid's breathing had grown heavy.

"I did," she said. "I heard something."

Goldie turned around. "What?"

"Like an engine revving really hard down the street."

Goldie nodded. "That's exactly what I heard." She looked at David. "It's probably just a passing truck, but do you think we should continue?"

Lilly couldn't help but make a grab for David's hand, full of worry for her daughter's safety. She had to keep Astrid safe at all costs, and he was her rock.

"I see the two officers in the lot," he said, holding up a hand in a waved greeting. "And there's a police vehicle parked across the incoming ramp to prevent anyone entering. I think we're safe to continue." He slid his hand from Lilly's and took his weapon from its holster. "High alert from here on."

Goldie led them out into the lot, more brightly lit than the stairwell, its strong odor of oil and grease enveloping them as they walked. The uniformed officers positioned themselves close to the agents' black SUV, parked in the corner directly beneath a security camera.

"We've swept the car for explosives," one of the officers said, approaching David. "It's clean."

Lilly felt Astrid stiffen beside her, slowing her pace. Then she stopped dead and held her hand in the air, just as Goldie had instructed.

David was instantly at her side. "What is it, Astrid? Do you see something?"

She tilted her head, turning her ear upward. "No, but I hear something. It sounds like a speeding car and it's getting louder."

In the next moment there was an enormous rev of an engine and a squeal of tires before a huge bang reverberated through the lot as a truck came crashing through the wall next to them.

David had no time to think. The truck appeared so suddenly that he was blindsided. The huge yellow vehicle broke right through the wall and came to a stop, smoke and brick dust billowing around the tires. This was a dump truck, solid and sturdy, capable of taking the kind of punishment that a brick wall can inflict. And behind the wheel was a masked man, presumably Henderson, shaking his head, ridding himself of the dizziness that must've affected him after the force of the impact.

Each member of law enforcement drew their weapon, shouting for the man to exit the vehicle and put his hands in the air. Within seconds, they were joined by the two officers who had been guarding the front entrance of the building, making a total of six weapons now trained on the truck. Surely the odds were in their favor?

Not necessarily.

"Goldie," David yelled, noting that the engine was revving hard once more. "Get Lilly and Astrid out of here. Now!"

Goldie didn't need to be asked twice. She grabbed Lilly by the sleeve of her sweatshirt and yanked her out of what appeared to be a dazed and terrified stupor.

"Follow me," Goldie said. "Quickly."

But the truck was moving, its enormous wheels rolling over the broken bricks and mortar in an effort to head their way. David's heart leaped into his mouth. Lilly and Astrid were directly in its path.

"Take him down," he yelled to the officers. "Do whatever you have to."

The entire parking lot was filled with gunshots as all weapons were aimed at the windshield and tires, firing round after round. Yet the truck didn't stop. With a shattered windshield and deflating tires, it careened toward them, swerving at the last minute to follow the path of Lilly and Astrid.

"No!" David shouted, running after the truck as it picked up speed. "Lilly, watch out!"

She turned, an expression of horror falling on her face. Goldie pushed her and Astrid between two parked vehicles and fired her weapon at the windshield of the truck repeatedly, diving from its path with only a second to spare. The huge yellow hood rammed into the small compact that was shielding Lilly and Astrid, and David heard a woman cry out. He tore to their location, praying neither of them was hurt.

Meanwhile, the truck was reversing, crashing into the cars behind it, narrowly missing Goldie lying on the ground. The officers raced toward the vehicle with weapons raised.

That's when it became apparent this dump truck wasn't the only weapon Henderson would be using that evening. Gunshots rang out from the truck's cab, hitting two of the officers, who sank to the floor, calling out in pain. David was torn, wishing he could rush to everyone's aid, but his main concern had to be placed on Lilly and her daughter. They were his priority and he must find them. As he ran, he yelled into his radio, "Agent David McQueen requesting a SWAT team at The Phoenix Apartment Complex, Pittsburgh. Immediately."

While more gunshots filled the air behind him, David reached the battered little compact and shouted Lilly's name. A hand grasped his leg from below, causing him to jump in alarm and point his gun to the target.

"It's me," Lilly said, her grime-streaked face peeking out from under the car "We're okay."

He squatted down and pulled her and Astrid from their hiding place. "Run hard and fast to the SUV," he said breathlessly. "I'll be right behind you."

"My legs," Astrid said, close to tears. "They're like jelly. They won't work properly."

"Dig deep, Astrid," he said, pushing her toward the car. "I know you can do it. You're strong. Go!"

He watched them run to the vehicle, Astrid being dragged along by her mother, the teenager's long legs almost buckling beneath her. He ran after them, hearing the gunshots die away and the sound of a revving engine fill the air instead. Goldie's voice called out across the lot, loud and panicked.

"David! He's coming for you."

He picked up his pace, noting that there were no parked cars between him and their SUV. There was no place to hide and nowhere to shield himself. The grating sound of the truck's engine was nearing but Astrid was slowing.

"Move faster, Astrid," he yelled, turning and firing the last of his bullets into the engine. Steam and smoke began to pour through the grille. "You're nearly there."

But she could go no faster and he caught up with her in a matter of seconds, just in time to fling her and her mother from the path of the moving dump truck and take the force of the impact in their place.

Lilly screamed in terror as she watched David bounce off the front of the truck and fall to the ground, rolling over and over until he came to a stop against a wall, where he remained, slumped in a heap. The truck halted in its path, engine screeching and straining while white vapor leaked through the hood. David's bullets seemed to have seriously damaged the mechanics, and the truck's engine finally cut out, leaving nothing but the hiss of the steam in the silence.

Then the cab door slowly opened and a foot appeared in the air, possibly readying itself to jump to the ground.

"Mom!" Astrid shouted, pulling on her mother's sweatshirt. "We have to get in the car."

Lilly wished she had a gun, a way to protect her daughter, but she was without a weapon. And without hope. The SUV was just a couple of yards away, but she didn't have a key to drive it. They'd be sitting ducks.

Then she caught sight of Goldie, running to their rescue, her mane of red hair flying like fire behind her. And she was closely followed by the two uniformed officers.

"Put your hands in the air," Goldie yelled, pointing her gun at the suspect. "You're under arrest."

The masked man jumped from the cab, immediately firing a weapon, causing everyone to dive for cover, including Lilly and Astrid. They clung to each other on the concrete, hidden beneath the SUV, Lilly uttering words of prayer while her daughter whimpered in her arms. Lilly saw black-clad legs streak past them and vault the wall by their SUV, disappearing from sight.

"Let him go," Goldie said to the officers. "We're out of ammo and it's too dangerous to engage him. I hear sirens coming our way, so let's hope the SWAT team finds him."

Lilly let go of Astrid and crawled on her belly out into the open. "Didn't you just point your gun at him? And you had no bullets in it?"

"Yeah," Goldie said with a raised eyebrow. "But he didn't know that, did he?" The smile faded from her lips as she looked around the lot. "Where's David?"

Lilly stood shakily, her legs struggling to hold her weight. "He's over there." She pointed to the slumped figure, which by now was thankfully moving and groaning. "He got hit by the truck."

Goldie holstered her weapon and turned to the officers. "You two, go stay with your wounded colleagues until the ambulance arrives. I'll see to David."

Lilly and Astrid followed Goldie to David's position and all three knelt around him as he coughed and rubbed his chest. Lilly loosened his tie and wiped the blood from a cut on his lip with her thumb, while Goldie checked him over for broken bones.

"It's only scrapes and bruises," he said, waving both women away. "I don't know how I'm not dead, but I guess somebody's looking out for me. Where's Henderson?"

"He ran when the truck's engine seized, but I'm hoping the SWAT team spots him," Goldie said, helping David to his feet. "We've got two officers awaiting ambulances, but they were smart enough to wear vests so their wounds aren't fatal."

"What a relief." David nodded slowly. "That's a good result."

Astrid made a snorting sound and Lilly watched her face go from confused to sad to angry in a matter of seconds. And she knew what was coming next.

"You can't be serious?" Astrid said. "Two policemen have been shot, you were run down by a truck and the bad guy just escaped without a scratch. How is that a good result?"

David smiled as if he understood where she was coming from.

"We're all alive," he said, continuing to massage his ribs gently. "That was a ferocious attack, which could've killed any one of us, but we're okay. I never thought I'd survive a collision with a thirty-ton dump truck, but I did, and I'm grateful."

"Grateful?" Astrid questioned. "I think you're crazy."

By now, numerous police vehicles had arrived outside the apartment complex and officers were making their way through the huge hole in the wall, their faces showing disbelief at the carnage that had been created in the parking lot.

"Now that the cavalry has arrived, I'd like to take a quick moment to give thanks for the fact we're all safe and well," David said. "If everyone is okay with that."

As expected, Astrid was very vocal in her objection. "Actually, I'm not okay with it." She turned to her mother. "I'm gonna get in the car, okay?"

Lilly led Astrid a few feet away. "You don't have to say anything, honey. Just close your eyes and listen."

"If you want to say thank you to some big bearded man in the sky, then go right ahead, but leave me out of it."

"You're in shock, Astrid," Lilly said, wrapping her arms around her daughter and cradling her head. "And it might help you to be quiet and still for a moment or two."

Astrid pushed her mother away. "I don't want to be quiet and still, Mom. I want to go home and go to school and see Noah." Her shock and anger were clearly keeping the tears at bay for now. "Praying to God won't make that happen, will it? It's stupid and pointless." She began to walk to the car. "I just want to go home."

Lilly glanced back at David and Goldie. "I'll sit in the car with Astrid and calm her down," she said. "Thanks for taking care of us today. I appreciate it."

She walked to the SUV, the adrenaline fading in her legs. She was exhausted, on the verge of tears and terrified of what might happen next. Astrid may feel that prayer was pointless, but in her position of fear and hopelessness, Lilly's faith was the only thing sustaining her. And she intended to cling to it for all she was worth.

David sat gingerly at the table, holding his bruised ribs. After being checked over by a paramedic, he had been given painkillers and an ice pack for the swelling and told to rest. The painkillers and ice pack were certainly helpful, but resting was not an option. He would need to work harder than ever now to ensure they were not being tracked by a mole inside the FBI.

Goldie removed the lids from numerous trays of Chinese food on the table in the new safe house apartment and handed everyone a plate.

"I'm sorry to have to tell you that Henderson hasn't yet been found," she said. "But I've asked all the local businesses to hand over their security footage so our tracing agents can track his movements from the apartment complex. It's weird how he manages to vanish into thin air."

"It's even more weird to be eating dinner at ten thirty," Astrid said, helping herself to the food. "But literally everything is weird lately."

"Hold up, Astrid," David said, clasping his hands together. "Let's say grace, first."

She put down her fork. "Oh, yeah, right. We have to talk to your imaginary friend before we do anything."

David bristled at her display of insolence. "Do you think you could show a little respect, just for five minutes? This is important to me."

He saw the pervasive roll of the eyes. It was little wonder that Astrid's eyes were not permanently damaged from all the rolling. Lilly reached out and placed a hand on her daughter's forearm to presumably quiet her. It didn't work.

"Just because it's important to you doesn't mean it has to be important to everybody." Astrid picked up her fork once again and started to eat. "You can live your life by your rules and I'll live by mine. Okay?"

David rubbed at his forehead. How on earth did someone so young manage to get under his skin to this extent?

He looked at Lilly. "Are you going to stand for this?"

Lilly appeared exhausted, as if she wanted to sleep for a hundred years. "We've been through a terrible ordeal this evening and I really don't want to fight." She tucked her blond hair behind her ears and clasped her hands together. "Say grace and let's eat."

"But Astrid has already started."

Lilly sighed. "Does it really matter?"

"Yes, it does." David didn't want to fight either, but something propelled him toward that destination. "I asked her to wait."

Astrid stood quickly, causing her chair to fall to the floor behind her. "I'm going to eat in my room." She picked up her plate and stalked off down the hallway. "I need some peace and quiet."

After her door slammed behind her, the three adults around the table remained silent for a few seconds.

"Well, it's nice that we're all getting along, huh?" Goldie said, reaching down to right the fallen chair. When neither David nor Lilly responded, she followed up with, "Sorry. I have an amazing talent for making bad jokes." She began to help herself to noodles. "Don't let this food go cold, guys."

"Are you simply going to ignore Astrid's behavior?" David asked Lilly, knowing it was not his place to demand that she return to the table but wishing he could. "She's totally unacceptable."

"Yes, I know." Lilly's voice was small and defeated. "Astrid is rude and offensive and awful. But she almost got killed today and she's dealing with some pretty intense emotions, so I'm going to let this one slide. I'll speak to her before she goes to bed and explain why she needs to consider other people's feelings before her own."

David knew that his own intense emotions were being influenced by memories of Chloe, but he couldn't help himself. The regrets and concerns fueled his words.

"Does she always reject God like that?" he asked. "Surely your church must give her guidance and support?"

Lilly pinched the bridge of her nose. "Astrid stopped going to church a year ago. She says she doesn't enjoy it."

David's mouth dropped open. Astrid was exactly like Chloe, turning her back on church, deciding her own rules, thinking she knew better than anybody else.

"Why don't you make her go?" he asked. "That would be the wisest thing to do."

"I disagree," Lilly replied. "I can't force her to believe the same things as me. Faith can only be true if it's freely given, and Astrid isn't quite ready yet." Lilly smiled, yet it didn't hide her pain and worry and vulnerability. "Give her time. She'll see the truth soon enough."

A sense of dread sank into David's stomach. He had thought the same thing about Chloe, assumed she would see sense and return to their church when she was ready. He had allowed her to skip the Sunday services and lounge in bed, giving her the freedom to make her own adult choices. He often wondered whether Chloe's rejection of God had meant she'd lost His protection over her. And the results of her disobedience were all too clear to see.

"What if Astrid doesn't have time?" he said. "She has no idea what's around the corner, so she could be placing herself in tremendous danger by refusing to accept God's hand."

Lilly fixed him with a stare that was as steely as it was sad.

"Astrid is a lost sheep," she said. "And I think God loves the lost sheep just as much as the ones already in His care."

He was silent for a moment, hearing only the sound of Goldie's knife and fork on the plate.

"Come on, guys," Goldie said encouragingly. "Stop talking and start eating."

But David wasn't hungry. He couldn't get Chloe and Astrid out of his mind. Was Lilly right? Did God also protect the lost sheep, as well as the found? He couldn't be sure, not while Chloe was preparing to stock shelves in a grocery store rather than pull on a doctor's white coat. He didn't want the same thing to happen to Lilly's daughter.

"I still think you're making a mistake," he said, deciding to err on the side of caution. "You should lay down the law with Astrid and force her to attend church."

"Just exactly what happened in your life to make you so obsessed with setting rules for Astrid?" Lilly challenged. "I'm guessing it's got something to do with your own daughter."

"Yes, it does," he said. "But I don't want to talk about it."

Lilly rose from the table. "Fine. Then I don't want to talk about my daughter either. I'll go sit with her while she eats. She needs my support after such a horrible day."

She lifted her chin and walked from the room, leaving David slightly shamefaced.

"I totally messed that up, didn't I?" he said to Goldie. "Why didn't you stop me?"

His partner laughed. "I tried my best, but you're kind of hotheaded when you want to be."

"Yeah, I guess I am, but you know why." Goldie was like a sister to him, someone who knew his entire life story. "I mean well."

"I know you mean well, David, but why would you expect Lilly to share her personal life with you when you're not prepared to do the same with her?"

He was slightly taken aback. "You think I should tell her about Chloe?"

"Yes, I do." She gave him one of her looks. "It's obvious that you like Lilly. Why don't you let her in a little bit?"

"No way. I'm fine just as I am, thank you." He took a forkful of noodles to busy himself. "Besides, I don't like her in that way."

"You're a terrible liar." Goldie stood up. "I'll go sit with the girls and give you some time to think about things. Pray about it, maybe."

Then she was gone and he was alone, dismissing her advice instantly. He didn't need to think about things and he certainly didn't need to pray about it. He was more than happy to risk his life for Lilly, but he absolutely, resolutely refused to risk his heart, as well.

FIVE

Lilly emerged from her bedroom the following morning to find David and Goldie carrying out yet another sweep of their new Pittsburgh apartment. Both agents had checked it thoroughly upon arrival the previous evening, but neither seemed able to fully relax without knowing how Henderson had discovered their former hiding place. In fact, nobody could relax. The atmosphere was tense for many different reasons.

"Good morning, Lilly," Goldie said brightly. "Did you sleep well?"

Lilly rubbed her eyes. "No. Astrid had a nightmare so I climbed in with her and she's not a great sleeping buddy." Lilly held her arms horizontally at her side, poker straight. "She sleeps like a starfish."

"Is she okay now?" David asked. He appeared to be remorseful in the wake of their argument. "Does she need anything?"

"She's fine." Lilly tucked her white blouse into the waistband of her jeans self-consciously. She didn't know how to talk to David. She so desperately wanted him to admire and respect her as a fellow parent, but not at the expense of her principles. "I think you two should clear the air when she gets up. She might be ready to apologize for lashing out."

David took a step into the kitchen, motioning for Lilly to follow.

"Actually, I owe you an apology too," he said, rubbing the back of his neck beneath his shirt collar. "I should've been a lot more understanding after what happened yesterday. We all needed to recover after the incident with the truck, and I upset you and Astrid with my heavy-handedness. I'm sorry. I'll try to be more laid-back from now on."

Lilly nodded slowly, indicating her acceptance of his remorse. The apology was certainly welcome, but she wasn't sure that would be the end of it.

"You're going to be more laid-back?" Was this even possible for someone like David? "That's a surprise."

He smiled. "Goldie thought I might benefit from being a little less uptight. And I think she's right."

Lilly glanced at his FBI partner in the hallway. "You and Goldie seem close." She was uncertain why she was heading down this particular avenue. "Are you two... um...an item?"

The expression on David's face told her everything she needed to know. He was obviously horrified.

"No! I mean, Goldie's a fantastic woman but she's like family to me." He laughed and whispered playfully, "And to tell you the truth, she terrifies me a little. She plays hardball."

Lilly laughed too, strangely pleased that there was no romantic connection between the two FBI agents. She had no idea why this news would be welcome, especially considering that she and David weren't exactly the best of friends. So why did she want to reach out and run her fingers through his hair? Why did she want to straighten his shirt collar and trace her finger along the neatly trimmed line of his beard? Clenching her fist, she dug her nails into her palm to rid herself of these images, telling herself that she was simply being drawn to his protection in their dangerous circumstances. That was all. A man was bound to hurt her in the end, so why let down her guard?

It was time to change the subject. "I'm guessing there are no more leads on Henderson's whereabouts?" she asked. "We still don't know where he is, huh?"

"The SWAT team searched the streets through the night, but he'd vanished. We've got agents reviewing as much security footage as possible to try and track his movements, but it's a slow process."

She thought of numerous agents sitting behind screens, working feverishly to pinpoint the villain's whereabouts. "Are you sure of who to trust? You said there might be a mole on the inside."

"That's a very real possibility. Henderson knew exactly where to find us yesterday, like he was tracking our location, and I have no idea how." David took a deep frustrated breath. "That's why we have to make sure that this apartment is clean. If someone has put a tracing signal here, we'll find it."

"How many people know our location?" she asked.

"Not many. Only a handful of the most trustworthy agents are responsible for sourcing our safe houses, which is why I can't get my head around the possibility that one of them is betraying us." His face grew darker. "But it wouldn't be the first accomplice Henderson has had. When he first started his criminal career many years ago, he was in the Army and he worked with a partner, who supplied him with drugs to sell on military bases."

Lilly was disbelieving. "Are you telling me that Henderson served his country?"

"The only person he truly wanted to serve was himself. After just one year in the Army, he was given a bad conduct discharge for possessing and supplying cocaine. When he'd completed his jail sentence, he turned to his drug dealing partner to help him create a more lucrative money-making enterprise."

"It sounds like they ramped up the stakes."

"Henderson's partner was smart and had a clean record so he joined the Philly Police Department and used its resources to identify potential victims for Henderson to kill and impersonate." David remembered the details as if it were yesterday. "They both took fifty percent of the profits and the dirty cop helped to throw the heat off Henderson during the subsequent murder investigations."

"You said Henderson works alone, so I guess something happened to his partner?"

"Yeah. He eventually got sloppy and made a mistake, which gave us probable cause to arrest him on suspicion of being an accomplice in two homicides. When he realized how bad prison would be for a disgraced cop, he cut a deal with the FBI and turned on Henderson." David dusted off his hands. "We thought the case was all sewn up. We arrested Henderson, assuming we had him bang to rights."

"What happened?"

"The cop ended up dead before we got to trial. He was murdered by another inmate."

"Do you think Henderson set it up?"

"I'm certain of it, but we had no way to prove it because no one would talk." David clenched his jaw. "Henderson walked free with a huge grin on his face and I've been waiting ten years to arrest him again. But he knows we need evidence and he never leaves any behind. He didn't show me his face when he ran your car off the road and he wore a mask yesterday. He gives us literally nothing to work with in terms of witnesses."

Lilly's shoulders sank as she remembered just how much pressure was weighing on them. The entire case hung on her. All of Henderson's future victims depended on her testimony, on her ability to stay alive and stop this monster from continuing his murderous rampage.

"Hey," David said, rubbing her upper arm. "You've gotten pale. I know this is scary, but I'll get you through it. Don't lose hope."

"I'm trying to stay positive, but what happened yesterday showed me how serious this guy is about killing me. He really, really wants me dead."

David continued the arm rubbing. "And I really, really want to keep you safe. I haven't lost a witness yet and I don't intend to start now."

"You've lost no witnesses? Honestly?"

"Honestly."

"Thank you," she said, raising a weak smile. "I know we don't agree on everything, especially where parenting Astrid is concerned, but I appreciate your care of us. It's important for me to say that." She shivered involuntarily, suddenly cold. "We need you."

"And I'm always here for you." He pulled her against his torso, rubbing her back gently. "You can rely on me."

Lilly breathed in David's citrusy aftershave scent, closing her eyes and letting her limbs relax one by one. But her peace was broken by Astrid padding into the kitchen in her pajamas and socks and staring at them openmouthed.

"That's gross," she said. "Nobody needs to see old people hugging."

Astrid took a carton of juice from the refrigerator and a glass from the shelf, then left the room. David pulled away from Lilly, showing a surprising resolve to stick to his new rule by smiling and shrugging in a laid-back way.

"Old people?" he questioned playfully. "Did she really call us old people?"

Lilly was pleased to feel a laugh rise from her belly, the first one in a long time.

"Yes, she did, but anybody over the age of twenty-five is ancient to her."

"Well, actually I'm only twenty-four, so she's in for a..."

He stopped mid-sentence as a wailing sound filled the kitchen, a high-pitched screech that flooded Lilly's senses with panic and dread.

It was the fire alarm.

David almost collided with Goldie in the hallway as they both rushed to the front door to assess the situation.

"It could be a scheduled test," David shouted above the noise, peering through the spy hole. "Can you check please, Goldie?"

She nodded, slipping her cell from her pocket and walking into the kitchen, finger in one ear.

"What's going on?" Astrid appeared in the living room. "Is there a fire?"

"We're not sure, honey." Lilly went to her daughter's

side. "But you need to get dressed in case we have to go outside."

Lilly led Astrid into her bedroom and closed the door, leaving David to wonder just how to proceed. Was there a need to leave?

"It's not a scheduled test," Goldie said, returning from the kitchen. "The maintenance manager wants everybody to evacuate. The fire department is on the way."

Instinctively, David knew that evacuating the apartment was a bad idea.

"Let's give it a little while," he said. "The last thing I want to do is take Lilly and Astrid out into the open."

"That's better than being trapped in a burning building though, right?"

"I don't think there's a fire." He sniffed the air. "It's almost certainly a false alarm."

"Do you think it's been triggered by Henderson to flush us out?"

"I don't know." David felt an acute pressure to make the correct decision. "I just don't know."

Goldie checked her watch. "I recommend we give it three minutes, and if the alarm is still sounding, we'll leave. But it's your call."

"That's a good plan," he said, turning the locks to open the front door. "I'm going to check the area. Stay here with the door locked and I'll be back in three minutes."

He slipped out into the hallway, which was deserted after other residents had presumably left the building. The cacophony was even louder in the corridor and he took his gun from its holster as he walked along the carpet, skirting the wall, knowing he would never hear an attacker coming up from behind. He strained to listen for the sound of movement behind the apartment doors, checked the empty elevator, raised his nose in an attempt to sniff out any smoke.

Clangs and bangs began to emanate from the stairwell, barely audible above the screeching alarm but a certain sign of someone in the complex.

Approaching the stairs, he checked his watch, noting that almost two minutes had passed. He would need to maintain careful timekeeping in order to ensure that Lilly, Astrid and Goldie didn't become trapped by a potential fire. Lilly's perfume still lingered in his nostrils, having transferred onto his shirt after their embrace, and he tried to put her out of his mind. Becoming too close to a witness in his care was dangerous, and he knew it would affect his ability to do his job. He couldn't quite work out how Lilly had snuck into his thoughts so frequently. They exchanged far more words in argument than agreement, so exactly why was he so keen to spend time in her company?

A clash resounded up the stairs, followed by a shout.

"Who's there?" he called, peering over the edge of the stairwell. "Identify yourself."

The alarm suddenly ceased, leaving behind a tinny ringing in David's ears. He shouted again.

"Who's there? I'm a federal agent."

A reply came from somewhere below. "It's the fire department just checking things out. Looks like a false alarm."

He didn't want to take any chances. "I'm coming down where I can see you."

He holstered his weapon, but kept his fingers curled on the handle, and began walking down the stairs. After two flights he was met by several firefighters, fully kitted out, two with hoses rolled over their shoulders.

The fire chief pointed to a smashed alarm activator on the wall. "Somebody set it off on purpose," he said. "But it looks like a malicious report because we can't find a fire." His eyes dropped to the weapon on David's belt. "Did you say you're a federal agent?"

"Yeah." He had to think quickly. "I'm here visiting my elderly mother."

"Well, you can tell her not to panic. We'll spend another hour or so making sure there's no danger, but experience tells me it's probably some kids up to no good. It happens sometimes."

David wanted to believe that this was the work of delinquent kids, but it seemed too much of a coincidence. He checked the stairwell for security cameras. None.

The chief turned to his colleagues. "Okay, guys, let's split up and carry out the necessary checks." He stopped, leaned over the handrail and called down to a masked firefighter lingering at the bottom of the stairwell. "Hey, you! Get your butt up here for job detail."

But the uniformed man instantly vanished, slipping through the exit door without acknowledging the order. David's eyes snapped to the large stairwell window overlooking the parking lot, to watch the guy ambling across the asphalt. Something about this man's flat-footed gait was eerily familiar. Henderson walked in exactly the same way, and David's heart lurched.

The chief shrugged, counting his men with an extended finger. "He must be from the South Side station. They arrived just after us."

David's stomach twisted into a vine of knots, doubting that the masked firefighter really was from the South

Side station. It was likely Henderson, attempting to blend in with the fire department to move freely through the building and seek out his targets. And this could only mean one thing.

They had been found yet again.

David reentered the apartment, looking pensive and strained, as if a million different worries were running through his mind. Lilly and Astrid were standing in the living room, both dressed and with bags packed, ready to leave immediately.

"The alarm stopped," Goldie said. "Did you find out what happened?"

When David failed to respond, she clicked her fingers in the air. "Hey! What's up? Talk to us."

"Sorry." He seemed to snap out of his trance. "It's a false report. The fire department is checking the building to make sure there's no danger, but it looks like somebody set off the alarm on the third floor without good reason."

Lilly squeezed Astrid's hand. "Do you hear that, honey?" she said with fake cheer. "It's a false alarm so you can go back to your room and unpack your things."

Astrid wasn't that easily placated. "But who set off the alarm?" she said. "It could've been him, right? It could've been Henderson?"

Lilly didn't want Astrid to know about the dread that had gripped her, so she took a deep breath and plastered on a smile.

"And it could've been a bunch of bad kids who think it's funny to waste the fire department's time." She pinched Astrid's cheek. "Which one do you think is more likely?"

"Henderson," Astrid said flatly. "Without a doubt. Stop trying to protect me, Mom."

"There's a very good chance that it was Henderson who activated the alarm," David said, ruining Lilly's plan to shield Astrid from the truth. "And I think he was masquerading as a firefighter to try and entice us out, but he got scared off when a fire chief challenged him."

"Should we leave?" Goldie asked.

"Not yet. He clearly doesn't know our exact apartment, so let's stay put for now and get some extra police patrols in the area. It's the least risky option at this stage, because we've seen what can happen when we go out into the open."

"I'll go organize the extra patrols," Goldie said, leaving the room, cell in hand.

Astrid clasped her hands together anxiously. "I think we should leave now. We shouldn't be taking chances. It's too dangerous."

Lilly exchanged a glance with David. Astrid was wound up tight. But it was little wonder she was afraid, considering that a huge truck had tried to run her down not long ago.

"I know you're scared," Lilly said, running her fingers through Astrid's long hair. "But you're safe here with us."

"You can't really believe that," Astrid shot back. "This guy is like a supervillain."

Lilly thought she would try to inject a little humor. "Does that make David the superhero?" Her joke fell flat.

"No, it doesn't," Astrid said. "He's not a comic book hero."

"That's a shame," David interjected. "Because I look fantastic in tights."

Both Lilly and David began to laugh. David seemed to instinctively know when to introduce a little lightheartedness, perhaps because he had raised two children of his own.

"I can't believe you two are actually laughing," Astrid said, folding her arms. "Somebody is trying to kill us and you think it's funny."

"Trust me, I don't think it's funny," Lilly said. "But we can't live in fear every second of the day. It's not healthy. We have to trust that everything will be okay."

"I'd rather trust my own judgment if it's all the same to you. I want to go home. I want to see Noah and go back to school. I want to stop being scared of every little creak I hear at night." She let out a moan of frustration. "I want to get back to normal."

"We all do," Lilly soothed. "Just hold on for a few more days."

Astrid's eyes pleaded with her mother. "Why can't I leave without you? Henderson would never know I wasn't here. I could sneak out in the middle of the night and go stay somewhere else, somewhere with Wi-Fi and all the movie channels."

Lilly was floored for a second or two. Did Astrid really want to split up at this most dangerous time of their lives?

"But where would you go?" she asked.

Astrid stared down at her feet. "I could go stay with Dad for a while."

Lilly really didn't want to revisit this conversation. "I already told you that he's on vacation. He's in Florida right now with his family."

Astrid's face fell at the mention of her father being with his family. After all, Astrid herself was his family, yet he spent next to no time with her.

"But if you called Dad and made him see how serious my situation is, he'd go back home to California right away and let me stay there with him until this is all over." Even Astrid didn't appear to fully believe her own fantasy. "He would want to look after me and keep me safe. All you have to do is ask."

Lilly and David were silent, neither of them wishing to address the elephant in the room. They both knew that Rylan would worm his way out of responsibilities, claiming a lack of time or resources.

Finally, it was David who spoke. "I think your mom and I would rather you stayed here with us."

A shiver fell down Lilly's spine to hear David say *your mom and I*. He phrased their situation as though they were a family, a tight-knit, happy family with two loving parents. And she liked it, however much she told herself not to.

"You only want me to stay here so you can order me around like you did with your own kids," Astrid challenged. "You want to turn me into a Goody Two-shoes, who obeys your every command."

"Astrid, stop it," Lilly said, her stress levels rising. "You can't leave the safe house because Henderson might come looking for you. I won't allow it."

Astrid obviously had another theory behind her mother's reluctance. "Is it because you don't want me to spend any time with Dad? Are you worried I might want to move to California and live with him instead of you?"

Lilly pushed the heels of her hands into her eye sockets. She couldn't keep going over this same old ground time after time. "No, that's not true. I'm worried that your dad wouldn't take care of you properly. I don't trust him to keep you safe, not like David does."

"That's a chance I'm prepared to take," Astrid said, turning to David. "Can we call him?"

"No."

"How dare you stop me from calling my dad," she said, her color rising. "You're overstepping your boundaries." This was clearly Astrid's attempt to sound grown-up and persuasive. "It's not your job to interfere in my family life."

"I used to know a girl like you, Astrid," David said calmly. "She was rude and difficult and thought she knew it all. I wish I'd had the courage to be straight with her, to tell her the truth about her deadbeat boyfriend and how he was no good for her. But I let her down because I gave her too much freedom. I thought I was giving her independence, but I was actually hurting her, because she never saw the danger around the corner."

"What are you talking about?" Astrid questioned. "Why are you telling me this?"

"I don't want to repeat the same mistake with you. You need to know that your dad isn't the man you think he is. He's a shirker who doesn't deserve to have you as a daughter. I'm telling you this for your own good, to stop him hurting you any more than he has already."

"David," Lilly rebuked. "Astrid is right. You're overstepping, and I want you to stop."

"My dad is a good person," Astrid shouted. "He loves me, and if you call him up, he'd let me go stay with him for as long as it takes." She stopped, apparently expended of energy. "He loves me."

"Sure, he does, honey," Lilly said, seething with anger at David. "Why don't you go unpack and I'll join you in a couple minutes, okay?"

Astrid gripped the handle of her case and wheeled it

away without another word. When her bedroom door clicked closed behind her, Lilly rounded on David.

"What is your problem? What on earth makes you think it's a good idea to tell a teenage girl that her father is a shirker?"

"She needs to accept the truth, Lilly," David said. "She knows it in her heart anyway. It makes no sense to pretend that her father will look after her and protect her, because he won't."

"This is about your own daughter again, isn't it?" she asked. "Somebody she loved hurt her, didn't he? I'm guessing it was the deadbeat boyfriend you mentioned."

"Yes, it was, and every day of my life I regret not doing more to prevent it. I should've made Chloe see that he wasn't worth her time and effort, just like Astrid's dad isn't worth her time and effort either."

Lilly sighed. "I had hoped that you and Astrid would clear the air between you today, but it looks like the air just got significantly worse." She folded her arms. "I expect both of you to apologize to each other later. This can't go on."

He threw his arms in the air. "I'm trying to help you here, Lilly."

"Well, stop trying to help." She turned and stalked from the room. "So much for your new effort to be laid-back, huh?"

She walked to Astrid's bedroom door, took a moment to calm herself and knocked before entering. Glancing back, she saw David standing in the living room, shaking his head and raking his hands through his hair in apparent frustration.

She was secretly pleased to see his reaction, hoping that she had given him a lot to think about.

* * *

The hush of nighttime was always David's favorite part of day. It was when he enjoyed solitude and peace, communing with God and letting his troubles be cast away.

But tonight was different. Tonight, his troubles refused to be cast aside, and they needled away, reminding him that he had failed in his one most important job—keeping his daughter safe. He thought he had learned to live with Chloe's injuries, to accept her situation and move forward. But since meeting Lilly and Astrid, he realized he'd been dead wrong. He was nowhere near accepting the past.

His cell began to buzz on the dresser beside the bed and he peered at the display. It was Chloe.

"Hey, sweetheart," he said, putting her on speakerphone. "I was just thinking about you. It's late. Is everything okay?"

"It's not late, Dad," she said. "It's only ten thirty."

He laughed. "That's late for me."

"I would've called earlier, but Paul came over for coffee."

"Paul?"

"He works at the grocery store with me. I started today."

"Oh, right, your new job. How's it going?"

"I love it. It's so much fun and Paul makes me laugh by doing goofy dances and telling lame jokes."

Somewhere in David's belly, a seed planted itself and he knew it would only germinate worry. "So you like this Paul guy, huh?"

"Yeah, I do. He's sweet and kind and nice, and although he's only twenty-five, he's the assistant manager already. He's a hard worker." She was silent for a second. "He's nothing like Eric."

Eric had been the name of her previous boyfriend, the one who had lost his life through his own stupidity.

"Do you think the two of you might end up going out on a date?" he asked.

"Maybe. He's asked me to go to his church youth group and I said I'd think about it."

David smiled. This went quite some way to allaying his fears. "You don't need to think about it, Chloe. You should go."

"Dad," she said, using a tone of voice that reminded him of Astrid. "You know that I like to make my own choices."

"Oh, boy, I know that, honey," he said. "I'll let you think about it and make your own decision."

"Thanks." Someone in the background called out her name. "I gotta go. One of the other girls in the complex made popcorn and I want to get some while it's hot. I just called to let you know that my first day at work was awesome."

"That's good news. I'm proud of you."

"Love you, Dad. Bye."

Then she was gone and David was left to imagine Chloe, his beautiful, fiercely smart daughter stocking shelves while the assistant manager goofed around to make her laugh. This scenario wasn't meant to be her future and while she was happy, she surely must be disappointed on some level.

A soft knock sounded on the door. It certainly wasn't Goldie. She was never that subtle. It must be Lilly or Astrid, whom he had successfully avoided all day by claiming a need to catch up on paperwork. He didn't want to cause any more arguments than he had already. He had asked Goldie to relay all the important information from headquarters, namely that police patrols had been stepped up and they were doing all they could to find Henderson in the area.

"Come in," he called.

The door opened a little and Lilly stood in the gap, cradling a mug in her hands. She wore a toweling robe over flannel pajamas, and her skin was rosy and shiny, scrubbed free of makeup.

"Hi," she said tentatively. "Is everything okay with you?"

"Sure."

"You've been pretty busy all evening. I was hoping we could talk about the arguments we've been having. We can't go on like this. You know that, right?"

"It's a little late now," he said. "Let's get a good night's sleep first."

She nodded her agreement. "I heard you talking on the phone just now. Was it your daughter?"

"Yeah. It was Chloe. She wanted to tell me about her new job. And potential new boyfriend."

Lilly smiled. "Is he nice?"

"She thinks so, but her judgment has been known to be off in the past."

"I guess you want to pin this guy down and give him the daddy warnings, huh?"

He laughed. "Yes, I do, but that's not how it works anymore. Apparently, girls get to make their own choices these days." He held up a hand in case she thought he might be serious. "That was a joke, by the way."

"You're a great father, David. Whatever guilt you're

holding on to, you should know that you're a great father."

This silenced him, and he was surprised to feel a well of emotion bubble up inside. He had tried his best to do the right thing by his daughters, to raise them to be strong and righteous. Yet he never felt proud of the job he'd done. His sense of inadequacy haunted him.

"Thank you," he said after a while. "That means a lot to me."

"I'm gonna turn in now. I'm bunking with Astrid because she has nightmares."

"Goodnight, Lilly. Sleep tight."

"Goodnight, David."

She closed the door and he set a wake-up alarm on his cell for 6:00 a.m., checked his weapon and laid it on the dresser beside him, said a quick prayer for divine protection during the night and finally rested his head on the pillow. Closing his eyes on the day, he hoped for a quick capture of the man who was hunting them. This assignment needed to be over.

As quickly as sleep seemed to come, it was broken again by a sound that David had been dreading to hear.

The fire alarm was shrieking another warning. And this time, he smelled smoke.

SIX

David pulled a hooded sweatshirt and pants over his pajamas and rushed out into the hallway, weapon in hand. Goldie had already emerged from her room and was talking on her cell, one finger in her ear to lessen the noise.

"The maintenance guy says there's a real fire this time," she said. "Down in the basement. The fire department should be here soon."

This was the work of Henderson. David was sure of it.

"We gotta get out of here," he said to Goldie. "Can you arrange for the local patrol units to get here quick and escort us out of the area?"

"I'll find a quieter room."

Goldie rushed past Lilly just as she came out of Astrid's room, pulling her hair into a ponytail, bleary-eyed and confused. "What's going on? What time is it?"

David checked the clock. "It's just after 1:00 a.m. There's a fire in the basement and we need to vacate the apartment immediately. Leave all your belongings behind and someone will retrieve them later."

She looked down at her robe and slippers. "Can't we get dressed first?"

"There's no time. I want to be out of here before the

fire department arrives, so we only have five or six minutes at the most."

Lilly wrinkled her brows. "You're talking like they're the bad guys."

"That's exactly what I'm afraid of, Lilly," he said. "Henderson might be masquerading as a firefighter again, and if they're all wearing masks, we have no way of knowing who to trust." He pointed to her open bedroom door. "Go get Astrid and let's leave."

But Astrid was already one step ahead of her mother, emerging from the room fully dressed and eager to escape the danger.

"I only packed the essentials," she said pulling on her backpack. "I left everything else."

"Smart kid," David said. "Hold hands with your mom and keep your wits about you. We'll head for the car in the basement lot, but if access is blocked by the fire, we'll go out front and wait for the police. Got it?"

Both Lilly and Astrid nodded, finding each other's hands and gripping tight.

"Two local patrols are on their way to meet us in the lot," Goldie said, striding through the hallway purposefully. "ETA of three minutes. We all ready to go?" She approached the front door as someone knocked briskly from the other side, and she put her eye to the spy hole. "The fire department got here really quick. It looks like they're doing door-to-door checks."

She turned the locks just as David realized what she'd said and shouted, "Goldie! No! Don't do it."

It was too late. She had forgotten about Henderson's latest disguise, and once the door had been opened just a crack, it flew wide with a bang, kicked firmly by a firefighter's boot. Then Goldie was struck across the head with a baton, flung sideways into the wall with a yelp and knocked out by the blow. A figure dressed in a yellow-and-black firefighter's uniform and full oxygen mask stepped calmly over her.

David barely had enough time to draw his weapon before Henderson did the same and, three feet apart, they began a tense standoff.

Astrid screamed and Lilly whimpered, but David shielded them.

"I just want the woman and the girl," Henderson said from behind his mask. "Give them to me and I'll let you live."

David narrowed his eyes to better see the face behind the breathing apparatus. As usual, Henderson had gone to great lengths to obscure his identity, making it impossible for David to accurately identify him.

"Lilly," David said, not moving his eyes off Henderson. "Take Astrid into the bathroom and lock the door. Make a barricade with whatever's there. Don't worry. I'll come for you soon."

They vanished without a word, while Henderson inched slightly to his left to watch their departure along the hall, his agitation growing. Both men maintained their weapons on each other throughout, aiming at the head, concentration unwavering. Meanwhile, the alarm continued its high-pitched wail, heightening the tension between them.

"You're making a big mistake," Henderson said. "You're gonna end up dead too."

"So shoot me," David replied. "You'll be dead before I hit the ground, I can promise you that."

"Give me the women." Each word seemed to be spat. "Now."

"Take off your mask, Gilbert." If Henderson revealed his identity, David could file another charge against him, one of assault against Goldie. But without that definite identification, the charge would never stick. "Let me see your face."

"Give it a rest, McQueen." The voice held a hint of a smile. "Don't be a hero."

The men began to skirt the room. "You remember me, huh?" David said. "I was working your case when you had your partner murdered in jail ten years ago. I've been waiting a long time to put you away."

"And you'll be waiting forever, because I'll outsmart you every single time you get close. Hand me the women and I give you my word that I'll let you live."

David's hackles rose. "You're a coward and a thief and a pathetic excuse for a man. Back slowly out of the apartment and *I* will let *you* live. How about that?"

Henderson laughed. "There's only one thing I hate more than cops, and that's FBI agents, especially the self-righteous ones."

"I'll take that as a compliment."

Voices began to sound in the main hallway of the complex, fire officers calling out to residents, knocking on doors, urging them to evacuate.

"This the fire department," someone yelled above the alarm. "Please vacate your apartments immediately. This is not a drill."

Henderson looked to the door, back at David and to the door again, seemingly assessing his options. Goldie murmured on the floor, turning over on the carpet and bringing her hand to her head in grogginess.

"This is your last chance, McQueen," Henderson said. "Step aside and give me what I want."

David simply took a step forward, his gun nearing Henderson's forehead. "I'd rather take a bullet."

In his peripheral vision, he saw a firefighter appear in the doorway, standing in apparent confusion, looking down at Goldie on the carpet, at the door kicked off one of its hinges and finally at the standoff in the living room.

"What the...?" he began.

In a split second, Henderson made a break for the door, shoving the firefighter roughly aside and running out into the corridor. David gave chase, determined not to allow him to escape, not again.

"There are two women and a teenage girl in that apartment," he called to the firefighter as he ran. "Evacuate them and take them to the nearest police officer."

He then trained his sights on his nemesis, whose heavy clothing and mask made his pace slow and clumsy. Henderson stopped at the stairwell, turned and fired a shot, causing David to dive to the floor. He then disappeared through the door.

David scrambled to his feet and raced after him, pushing the door with his shoulder and raising his weapon. Just ahead, he saw a flash of yellow and black disappear down the stairs and vaulted the bannister to cut him off. He practically landed on top of the running figure, knocking him to the ground in a twist of limbs.

"What do you think you're doing?" a voice yelled. "Get off me."

David leaped to his feet. This guy wasn't Henderson.

"I'm so sorry, sir," he said, offering a hand to assist him to stand. "I thought you were someone else." He produced his badge. "I'm an FBI agent. Did you just see a man dressed as a firefighter come this way?"

The man stood, straightened his jacket. "The whole building is filled with men dressed as firefighters, and we need to be able to do our jobs without being attacked. The basement fire is small but we're evacuating as a precaution. Step aside please, sir, and do not interfere with our duties again."

David holstered his weapon, allowed the man to pass. "I apologize."

Running back up the stairs to the apartment, he knew he'd have to allow Henderson an easy escape. The firefighter disguise was all too perfect in an emergency situation. And while Goldie was injured, she could offer no defense to Lilly and Astrid.

His next course of action should involve figuring out who was feeding Henderson information about their whereabouts. It was time to accept that there was definitely a mole within the FBI.

Someone was betraying them.

Lilly sat on her bed, wondering whether it was worth unpacking her clothes in this third safe house. The stress of constantly moving around was beginning to take its toll, and the rings under her eyes told the whole story.

Astrid had been subdued too, still in shock after being confronted by a fake firefighter brandishing a gun. Yet David's fierce protection of them seemed to have given her a new admiration, and she had stuck close to him ever since. She was now in the enormous kitchen of their temporary home, a brand-new, detached house on a deserted cul-de-sac. It had never been lived in before and smelled of fresh paint and carpet. Astrid adored the house straight away, especially the kitchen gadgets, and had insisted on making breakfast, after which everybody would surely be ready to catch up on a lost night's sleep.

A knock sounded on the door and David stuck his head into the room. "Hey, you," he said. "You want some breakfast soon? Astrid is making a huge stack of pancakes."

"Sure." She forced a smile. "You two seem to be getting along well at last."

He came into the room. "I'm treading carefully but she's warming to me. She's gone a whole hour without calling me old."

She tried to smile at the joke. "Thanks for taking care of her, David. I've needed a little time to gather my thoughts."

He sat on the bed. "How are you feeling?"

"I'm okay. More importantly, how is Goldie?"

"She's as tough as they come, so she's doing fine. The paramedics said there's no sign of concussion and she's helping Astrid make the pancakes while they both dance around the kitchen with the radio on. It's helping them release some tension."

"That's good."

"And we got a decent lead on Henderson at last. The police found his hideout this morning, and it looks like he got out in a hurry because he left a lot of things behind, including a bunch of stolen IDs. That means we know his aliases and we can start to track each one. Hopefully one of them will strike gold."

She smiled. "That's even better news."

He took her hand, his palm soft and warm against her cold one.

"I know this is hard on you," he said. "And I give you my word that we've stepped up security procedures to make sure you stay safe. There are two FBI agents stationed in the empty house across the street, constantly watching and reporting back on any suspicious activity."

"But how do we know we can trust them?"

"I've known these guys for twenty years and I'd lay down my life for each of them. They'd do the same for me. We can trust them."

Lilly shifted to cover her face with her hands, gripped by the thought that they could shortly be moving again, destined to flee from place to place in an effort to escape a killer.

"Then who is giving us away?" A thought struck her. "Do you think it could be Goldie?"

"Absolutely not. Goldie is as honest as they come."

"I'm sorry for doubting her," Lilly said. "But this situation is making me paranoid. I'm not sure who to trust anymore."

He took her hand again. "You can trust me. You know that, right?"

Despite all the arguments and recriminations and bad feelings, Lilly knew with certainty that she could rely on this man. He had proven his goodness.

"Yes, I trust you. Implicitly."

"Great," he said. "And I trust you too."

She laughed. "Well, at least we agree on something."

"I think we agree on a lot of things," David said. "We just don't know how to show it."

Lilly was unconvinced. "What do we agree on?"

"We agree that children need love and guidance and good role models. We agree on working hard and providing for your family and taking responsibility for your own situation. We agree that faith gives us the strength to keep going when times are tough. We agree that bananas should be banned in all fifty states for crimes against taste buds."

She laughed and leaned against him. "I don't remember telling you that I hate bananas."

"Astrid told me. She also told me you love avocados, pink nail polish and swimming. Although not all at the same time."

Lilly narrowed her eyes. "Have you been pumping her for information?"

"No." He smiled. "Perhaps a little. You're a closed book sometimes."

She didn't know what to make of this. Was David interested in knowing more about her because he was assigned to protect her or was it something more? Either way, it was clear that Astrid had been spilling the beans.

"I guess I don't mind Astrid telling you things about me if it means the two of you can find a way to be friends," she said. "I don't think I can face any more arguments. I'm exhausted with it."

"I understand. I'm planning on having a long chat with Astrid and giving her a copy of the code of conduct that I talked about. I need to respect her boundaries and she needs to respect mine. How do you think she'll react?"

"I think she'll roll her eyes, say *whatever* and flounce into her bedroom."

"I don't mind that," he said. "As long as she takes a copy of our code of conduct with her."

Lilly turned serious, sensing that David was genuinely trying hard here.

"I know you're putting a lot of effort into building a better relationship with Astrid," she said. "Other men would simply walk away and write her off, but you're prepared to go the distance because you know how to be a good father." She saw the flare of his nostrils, the way he always pushed back against a fatherhood compliment. "Stop with the modesty. You have to learn to take the praise."

He released her hand and clasped both of his together, sighing deeply, shoulders sagging. He finally seemed ready to reveal his most guarded secret.

"My youngest daughter, Chloe, was always the brightest in her class," he said. "And she was determined to be a doctor, especially after her big sister graduated law school and passed the bar. Chloe wanted to work at Mercy Hospital in Pittsburgh, the place where her mother was treated with love and dignity in the days before she died of cancer. Chloe was so smart and caring, and I couldn't have been prouder."

Lilly noticed him brush away a tear. "What happened?"

"She met an older boy called Eric who was rebellious and cool and dangerous, and he managed to convince her that it was more important to party than study. She started staying out late, being rude, refusing to go to church, answering back whenever I challenged her."

Lilly could see the parallels. "A little like Astrid, huh?"

"Exactly. Except Chloe was worse, because she would lie to me all the time. Astrid may be badly behaved, but she seems to be pretty open and honest."

"Yeah," Lilly agreed. "I think she is."

"When I close my eyes at night, I still hear the knock at the door. I think police officers have a way of knocking that somehow lets you know it's bad news. I knew instantly that Chloe was in trouble." He rubbed his forehead with his thumb and forefinger. "And I was right. On that particular night, Eric had gotten drunk and hit a tree at seventy miles an hour with Chloe as a passenger. He hadn't been wearing a seat belt but thankfully Chloe was. It saved her life."

"Eric didn't make it?"

"He died instantly and Chloe suffered a massive head injury when a branch came through the windshield. She was placed in a medically induced coma for three months."

"Oh, David, that's awful. You must've been out of your mind with worry." Lilly couldn't imagine how she would feel if something like that happened to Astrid. "But she pulled through."

"She eventually began breathing on her own, so the doctors brought her out of the coma and conducted some tests." He swallowed away what sounded like a sob. "And it quickly became apparent that she wasn't the same person as before. She suffered severe brain damage that left her unable to take care of herself. It took two years of rehabilitation to get her walking and talking, feeding herself and living normally."

"But that's good news, right, because she overcame the injuries?"

"She'll never recover her intelligence," he said. "That's gone. Instead of training to be a doctor right now, she's working at a grocery store, stocking shelves. She's happy enough and seems to love the job but it's not what I wanted for her. That one decision to get in a car with her drunk boyfriend cost her everything. Her life is ruined because she didn't take my advice when I asked her to stop seeing Eric and knuckle down to her studies."

In that moment, everything became clear to Lilly—

David's frustration with Astrid, his insistence on following rules, his dogged determination to bring Astrid under control. He was trying to stop history repeating itself, hoping to prevent another promising young life from being ruined.

"It's not your fault, David," she said. "Chloe sounds like a strong-willed young woman and you did everything you could to show her the way."

"I didn't do enough," he said through gritted teeth. "I should've taken a firmer hand."

"You have to forgive yourself." Lilly placed a hand on his cheek. It felt natural to hold it there, cupping his face, the bristles of his beard rubbing her palm. "Chloe's life isn't over. It's simply taken a different path and she's still the daughter you always loved. You shouldn't let that one incident define either of you. Your daughter made a bad choice, but you are still a good, kind and decent father, who raised his girls to be strong and smart. I'm sure they're proud of you."

He looked intensely at her, his dark brown eyes glistening slightly in the early morning light from the window.

"It's hard to believe they're proud of me when I can't be proud of myself."

She rubbed a thumb across the cleft of his chin. "I'm proud of you. Perhaps that can be enough for now."

He smiled. "Really?"

"Really."

"It's been a long time since a woman has made me feel ten feet tall, but you just reminded me what it's like." He cupped her face, mirroring her position. "Thank you."

Lilly knew it was inevitable that their lips would gravitate together, drawn by the heady atmosphere in the room. All the arguments were suddenly forgotten and replaced with a mutual respect, a shared desire to know one another more intimately.

Lilly barely had more than five seconds to enjoy the soft warmth of David's mouth on hers when a creak on the floorboard in the hallway alerted her to a snooper. She snapped her head sharply toward the slightly open door just in time to see Astrid's long legs hightailing it down the stairs.

Putting her head in her hands, she said, "Astrid was in the hall, and I think she saw us kiss."

This would complicate David and Astrid's relationship more than Lilly cared to imagine.

Goldie helped David clear away the breakfast dishes and load the dishwasher. A padded dressing covered the cut on her forehead and Goldie occasionally pressed it with her fingers, securing the surgical tape firmly to the skin.

"Are you sure you're okay to continue working?" David asked. "Your health is more important than completing this assignment."

Goldie waved away his concern, as he knew she would. "It's nothing. Just a scratch." She glanced over her shoulder to where Lilly and Astrid were sitting in the living room, playing a card game and laughing together. "Besides, I've grown really fond of the kid. She's all right when you break through the hard shell."

"I think I might know what you mean," he said. "I'm still not totally through the hard shell, but I'm making progress."

Goldie shot him a coy look. "It looks like you made much more progress with the mom. What's going on with you two?"

"What do you mean?"

"There were a lot of long, lingering gazes over breakfast and Lilly touched your hand way more times than she needed." Goldie smiled. "You like each other. A lot."

David decided that honesty was the best policy here. "Yes, we like each other, but it's complicated and I'm working their case, so I should take a step back."

"If anyone deserves to find love again, David, it's you. When this is all over, I hope your relationship with Lilly works out for you, because she's exactly the type of woman you need to make you happy."

He smiled, unused to his FBI partner showing this level of emotion. She always said she didn't believe in love.

"Are you being slushy, Goldie? This is totally unlike you."

She laughed. "Don't get used to it. It's just temporary insanity."

"Listen," he said, his laughter now replaced with seriousness. "We need to find out how we're being found and who might be responsible. I want you to compile a list of agents who've had opportunities to access our safe house information. You'll need to dig deep, turn over every stone. We've tightened our security but it might not be enough to stop our mole."

Goldie shook her head sadly. "I've been working the bureau for ten years, and this is the first time I've ever had to investigate a corrupt agent. I can't believe someone would betray us."

"Let's not forget that Henderson had an accomplice once before, and he's stolen millions of dollars over the years, so he's able to offer big rewards for information.

Find out if any agents have been offered a bribe, but tread carefully. Don't let them know we're on to them."

"This is my favorite part of the job," she said, heading for the door. "I love to find the needles in haystacks. You need to get some sleep. I'll take the morning shift and wake you this afternoon."

She left the kitchen, passing Astrid, who was balancing two empty cups in one hand and holding a deck of cards in the other. Wearing a pastel pink sweater, she was uncharacteristically colorful today.

"Hi," David said, taking the cups to stack them in the dishwasher. "You look nice. What do you call it? A norm?"

Astrid sat on a stool at the kitchen counter and began to play Patience on the flat surface. "It's Mom's sweater. I like it because it smells of her perfume. But, yeah, I look like a norm."

He motioned over Astrid's shoulder to the couch in the living room, where Lilly was reclined. "How's your mom?"

"She fell asleep." Astrid yawned and stretched. "I'll turn in soon too."

He slid across a piece of paper sitting on the counter, being careful to avoid disturbing her cards.

"I'd like you to take a look at this," he said. "It's a code of conduct that I drew up, which should help us be more respectful to one other."

She took the paper, folded it four times and slid it into her jeans pocket. "I'll read it later."

Then she resumed her card game, falling silent, and David wondered if she wanted to broach the subject of the kiss she had witnessed between him and Lilly. She was continuing to turn the cards and place them on the counter, but she glanced his way every few seconds, as if working her way up to speaking.

Finally, he broke the ice. "Did you see me talking to your mom earlier? She says you were standing in the hallway."

Astrid put down the deck of cards. "Yeah, I saw and heard everything."

"And how do you feel about it?"

He braced himself for the unavoidable you-can't-replace-my-dad speech that she was entitled to make, but she totally surprised him with something else entirely.

"I think that Chloe sounds awesome," she said. "She fought really hard to recover after the car accident and you don't seem to give her any credit for it. All you feel is disappointment because she's not a doctor."

He was blindsided by the criticism and stood in silence for a few seconds.

"I agree that Chloe is awesome," he said. "And I also admit that I'm disappointed. She had a lot of potential before the accident and it's been wasted. She could've had a successful life."

"What exactly is success?" she asked. "Does it mean having a great job with lots of money and a big house?"

"Sometimes," David replied. "It depends."

"It seems to me that Chloe is already successful," Astrid said. "She loves her job and she's happy with her life. I'm guessing that after all the rehabilitation she takes nothing for granted. She appreciates being able to walk and talk and laugh and stock shelves. It makes me angry that you're disappointed in her for not living up to your expectations of being a high-flying doctor."

"Now hang on, Astrid." He was beginning to become

defensive. "It was Chloe herself who had high expectations. She was planning on going to medical school."

Astrid stood up. "But did she really, truly want to become a doctor, or did you put pressure on her?"

He tried to think back to the time before the accident. Chloe had made her own choice to become a doctor. Hadn't she? He had perhaps steered her toward that career but not too heavily.

"I helped her make the decision to apply for medical school," he said. "But it was her choice in the end."

"Are you sure about that? Have you asked her?"

"No, I haven't asked her. I don't want to upset her."

Astrid began walking to the door. "I think you just don't want to hear the truth. I don't think Chloe ever wanted to become a doctor. She sounds like a free spirit who always wanted to live a simple life. But you wanted her to be someone different, and that's why she rebelled."

He had heard enough. "You're being presumptuous, young lady," he said. "Chloe chose to be a doctor because she was smart and wanted to help people."

"Smart people also work in grocery stores," she said feistily. "And they help people too. Maybe Chloe is living the life she always wanted, but you're too disappointed in her to see it."

"This conversation is done," he said, fighting to keep his cool. "Why don't you go to bed and get some rest? We're both tired and emotional this morning."

Astrid eyeballed him for a moment, as if weighing her options of challenging him or walking away. She thankfully decided on the latter.

"I also saw you kiss my mom," she muttered as she disappeared through the door. "Don't go thinking you'll be replacing my dad anytime soon."

* * *

David waited anxiously for Chloe to pick up, practicing the words in his head, wondering if he was doing the right thing. Was it best to leave this particular can of worms unopened?

"Hey, Dad," his daughter said brightly upon answering her cell. "I just got off work and I'm on my way home to get changed. I decided to go to the church youth group with Paul tonight."

"That's great news, honey. I'm really pleased." He took a deep breath. "I just wondered if I could ask you a couple of questions. Tell me if you don't want to talk about it and I'll stop. It's up to you, okay?"

"You can ask me anything, Dad. You know that."

He decided to come right out with it. "Did you always want to be a doctor? I mean before the accident."

She took a long time to respond. "No. *You* wanted me to become a doctor, but I didn't know what I wanted to be. I sort of still don't know."

A dull pain throbbed in his chest. How had he not seen this? "Did I put pressure on you to apply to medical school?"

Again, she waited before replying. "Yes, you did, but please don't feel bad about it. You wanted me to save people's lives and get a job at the same hospital where Mom died so I could be close to her memory. You thought you were doing the right thing."

This was hard to hear. "Is that why you rebelled? Was it because you didn't want to be pushed into a career you didn't choose?"

"Kind of." He could hear her breathing with the rhythm of her gait, slightly lopsided due to the leg weakness that had resulted from the brain injury. "I can't bear the sight of blood, Dad, and I had no idea how I'd cope in medical school. I didn't know how to tell you, so I decided I'd show you that I wasn't such a good kid after all. It was easier to disappoint you than to fail at being a doctor."

"Oh, Chloe." He fought back the tears. "I'm sorry. I had no idea I was putting so much pressure on you. Can you forgive me?"

"There's nothing to forgive, Dad. I was a total nightmare and you did everything you could to help me, but I wouldn't open up to you. I'm the one who messed up. Anyways, things worked out great for me in the end, because I think I'm living the life I was meant to lead."

"You do?"

"You used to say that God gives us what we need but not always what we want. Do you remember?"

"Yes." Somewhere along the line, he had forgotten this important detail. "And it's still true."

"Of course it's true. I have everything I need. It's not much but it's plenty enough."

"Did I ever tell you how proud I am of the woman you've become?"

"Only a million times over, Dad. Don't worry so much about me. You taught me enough to know that life is meant to be enjoyed, and I'm loving every minute."

He closed his eyes, steadied himself. "Thank you for this chat."

"It's kind of come out of the blue," she said. "What prompted it?"

"A teenage girl who thinks I'm old and boring," he said with a laugh. "But she's clearly a lot smarter than I give her credit for."

"She sounds like an interesting character. I see my

bus coming around the corner so I gotta run. I love you, Dad."

"Love you too. Say hi to Paul for me."

He hung up the phone, placed it in his pocket and clasped his hands together to say a prayer of thanks, of repentance, of acceptance and grace. Chloe had shown him that fatherhood was a continuous learning process, a position of constant growth. And he was humbled by her forgiveness.

That was when the alarm unit clipped to his waist began to bleep, relaying a warning from the agents in the house across the street.

Danger had found them.

SEVEN

It was late afternoon and Lilly was dozing on the sofa while Astrid played cards when David rushed through the living room, dropping the blinds and pointing her toward the stairs.

"Take Astrid into your bedroom and lock the door behind you." He handed her a gun. "Don't come out until I give the all clear. Got it?"

She was suddenly wide-awake. "Got it."

"What is it?" Astrid asked, following them into the hall. "Did something bad happen?"

"I don't know," he replied. "I got a danger warning from the agents across the street, so Goldie will stay here with you while I go check it out. It's only a yellow alert at the moment, so there's no need to panic." He touched Lilly's shoulder reassuringly. "Okay?"

Goldie appeared in the upstairs hallway, awoken from her nap. "I got the same alert, David. I'll lock up behind you and stand guard."

Lilly made a grab for David's hand, instinctively and naturally, holding it tight for a couple of seconds. She didn't want him to be hurt, especially now that they had grown so close. Astrid noticed the gesture of affection and pinched her lips in an expression of displeasure, folding her arms and stomping up the stairs, passing Goldie on her way down.

"We'll talk later," David whispered, withdrawing his hand. "Stay safe."

He walked to the door, turning and winking at her before leaving the house. Lilly's belly went into a kind of free fall just at the sight of that wink, and she gently reminded herself that she mustn't behave like a lovestruck teenager. She had been a love-struck teen when she'd met Rylan, overlooking his faults and quashing her misgivings because he sent her stomach into a swirl. Now a sensible woman in her thirties, Lilly needed to behave with more maturity, to protect both her and Astrid from another letdown. There were a ton of complications associated with any new relationship.

Skipping up the stairs after Astrid, Lilly could clearly see that the most serious complication was her daughter's feelings.

"There's no need to look so worried," she said, entering the bedroom and locking the door behind her. "David told us it's not a high alert."

"I think you should let me call Dad," Astrid said, sitting on the double bed and pounding a pillow with her fist. "If I go stay with him, you and David get to be all alone, just like you want to be."

Lilly knew exactly what had made her this upset. "You saw us kissing this morning."

"Yes, I did, and I can't believe you would be interested in a man like him, Mom."

"What do you mean—a man like him?"

"He's so straitlaced and boring." She punched the pillow again. "And he doesn't like me."

Lilly placed the gun on the dresser and sat on the bed next to her daughter. "Oh, honey, that's not true. I happen to know that he thinks a lot of you. You remind him of his own daughter."

"I already have a dad in my life, so I don't need another one, thank you very much."

Lilly fought back an urge to laugh. Astrid most definitely did *not* have a dad in her life, and hadn't for at least two years.

"David and I aren't serious about anything," she said gently. "We had one little kiss, so don't jump ahead of yourself."

Astrid turned her face away from her mother's, her voice growing thick with emotion. "I always kind of hoped that you and Dad would get back together." She wiped away a tear. "And now David has messed it all up."

Lilly put a flat palm on her chest in shock. There was no way she and Rylan would ever reconcile, and Astrid was living in a fantasyland if she thought otherwise.

"I was happy with your father for a little while," she said. "And you were born out of genuine love. But he moved on a long time ago and I think I deserve to be happy again too."

"Aren't you happy with me?"

"Of course I am." Lilly stroked Astrid's hair. "But in two years' time, you'll be making plans to go to college, perhaps far away from home. No matter how much I love you, I want someone else in my life."

Astrid's shoulders shrank down. "But David doesn't understand me, not like Dad does."

Lilly sighed. How could Astrid have forgotten all the terrible birthday presents Rylan had sent, proving that he didn't understand her at all? The doll she had gotten when she turned thirteen and was about to start high school. The secondhand bicycle with a broken bell. A purse that was bright yellow, the color she hated most in the world. These were hastily bought gifts, sent without thought, before he gave up trying completely. Now Astrid received nothing.

"Why don't you give David a chance?" Lilly said. "He wants you to like him and he's trying really hard."

Astrid groaned. "He's not trying hard at all. He just orders me around and treats me like a baby. I don't like him, and I don't want him in my life."

"What if I want him in mine?" Lilly asked.

"I'll run away and go to California to live with Dad."

"Astrid," Lilly said reproachfully. "Stop talking like that. For the time being, we have to trust David and follow his orders. I don't care if you don't like him. Your life is in his hands."

Astrid threw herself sideways onto the duvet, picked up White Bear and buried her head under the pillow. Lilly rubbed her back soothingly.

"Leave me alone," came Astrid's muffled voice. "Everybody hates me."

Lilly removed her hand and gazed down at her daughter's shoulders shaking slightly with her silent tears. No mother ever wanted to see her daughter in pain like this and Lilly would do anything to make it stop.

Perhaps it was time to let that mature woman in her thirties start calling the shots. She vowed to reel in her wayward emotions before she made another colossal mistake.

David walked across the backyard and vaulted the fence, before emerging onto the street via the pathway of the empty house next door. He then followed the directions of the agents standing in the window of the house opposite, pointing him toward a white van parked on the corner of the street. A man was standing at the open door at the back, leaning inside, only his blue pants and boots visible.

David unclipped his radio as he walked, keeping the other hand rested on his holstered weapon.

"What have we got?" he said quietly into the radio.

"A white male, about forty years old," came the reply from one of the agents inside the undercover house. "He's been scoping the street for a few minutes, walking up and down, looking into windows."

"Is it Henderson?"

"Negative."

Could this man be the new accomplice? David approached the van with caution, clipping his radio back onto his belt and covering his weapon with his jacket. If this person was in fact an innocent bystander, he didn't want to create a scene.

"Hi there," he said, tapping on the side of the van. "Do you need any help, buddy?"

The man stepped away from the van and straightened up. David resisted the urge to make a grab for his gun. His senses were heightened after the experiences of the last few days.

"Hello, sir." The man was smiling cheerfully, wearing a navy blue peaked cap on which the words *Green Fingers Florist* were written in red thread. "I'd sure appreciate your help actually."

David did a slow and complete turn on the sidewalk, taking in his entire surroundings. All was tranquil in this new residential development, with all of the houses in their little cul-de-sac empty and awaiting sale.

"Sure," David said, affecting a neighborly tone. "What do you need?"

The guy reached into his van and David put a hand beneath his jacket, ready to draw his gun at a second's notice. Yet the man simply pulled out a huge bouquet of flowers, wrapped in cellophane.

"I'm looking for a lady by the name of Lilly Olsen," he said. "There's no address on the card, only the name of this estate, so I'm not sure which house to knock. And they all look empty to me anyway."

David's heart rate hiked up a notch. "Lilly Olsen?"

"Yeah, you know her?"

David shook his head. "Never heard of her. I think you must have the wrong location. I'm the only resident on the street." He gesticulated to the for-sale signs in the front yards along the street. "The rest of these houses are unsold."

The man placed the flowers back into his van. "I have no idea why the store took the order without an exact address. Thanks for your help, buddy."

The guy closed the doors of the delivery vehicle, took his clipboard from the roof and sat in the driver's seat to write on the paperwork. As David turned and began walking away, he surreptitiously unclipped his radio and spoke into it.

"Watch this guy until he leaves, and then call a florist called Green Fingers to ask them who placed an order for delivery to Lilly Olsen. Get as much information as you can, because it seems to me that Henderson might know our general location but not the actual address. This is his way of pinpointing where we are."

He crossed the street, hiding his radio and waving to the delivery driver, deliberately walking along the side path of the wrong house in order to cut across the backyard and vault the fence into the yard of the safe house. He gave Goldie the fright of her life when he landed right in front of the kitchen window where she was standing guard looking pensive, gun in hand.

She opened the back door. "What did you find?"

"It was a florist trying to deliver flowers to Lilly."

"Henderson found us again?"

"He seems to know our general location," David said. "But I have no idea how."

"Actually," said Goldie. "Something weird happened earlier. I detected a transmission signal when I was doing a sweep of the house, but it was super quick, like only a few seconds. I assumed it was from a passing car, but it could've been something else."

"Could it have come from one of our phones?" David asked.

"The signals on both of our cellphones were already visible," Goldie replied. "But this new signal was an extra one, definitely inside or very close to the house."

This was a cause for concern, especially as passing cars are a rarity in a deserted cul-de-sac. "Something has given Henderson an idea of our safe house location, but he doesn't seem to be able to identify the exact house. Keep checking for signals, Goldie. I'll go update Lilly on what's happening."

David climbed the stairs, his mind running through all the ways that Henderson might be able to track them. Goldie's investigation had so far come up with nothing, no reason to suspect any agents of betraying them. Just what was going wrong?

He knocked lightly on Lilly's bedroom door, calling out the safe word. When she opened up, her face was pale and tense, as if the weight of the world had settled on her during the last few minutes. She smiled and touched his arm, sending a tingling sensation dancing across his skin.

"Is everything okay?" she asked, leading him out into the hallway and closing the door. "Astrid is pretty upset so I don't want her to hear any bad news."

He decided to keep things simple. "It's bad news but it's not terrible news. Henderson knows we're in this residential development, but he doesn't know the precise house."

She closed her eyes, exhaled loudly. "Do we have to leave?"

"Let's give it a little time. I'd rather stay inside and out of sight right now."

"That's good with me. Astrid needs some quiet time."

He touched Lilly's cheek but she turned her head away, and he wondered what had changed since that morning. He thought they'd made a connection.

"What's wrong?" he asked.

"Astrid saw us kiss and she's got this crazy idea that you want to take her father's place," she said. "I tried to talk some sense into her, but you know what she's like. She's stubborn and determined and she won't listen."

Lilly's posture was not inviting any affection from him, with her arms crossed tightly against her chest, her shoulders angled slightly away from him.

"She'll come around in time," he said. "It's natural for Astrid to want you all to herself. She's very close to you. Too close, perhaps."

"You think she's too close to me?" she asked. "In what way?"

He tried to backtrack. "It's great that you have such a strong relationship, but she makes a lot of demands on you." His backtracking was failing. "Perhaps it's time she learned that her mom is a person in her own right."

Lilly pointed to the door. "Astrid is in there cuddling a teddy bear that I gave her when she was two years old. She doesn't know how to see me as anything other than her mother at this moment in time."

"She's old enough to accept that you have a life separate from her," David said. "She's not a little girl."

"That's kind of the problem, David," she said. "Astrid is still a little girl in so many ways and she needs me to focus all my time and effort on her. I can't afford to make any mistakes or I might lose her."

"I understand why you're scared of hurting her feelings," David said gently. "But it's not fair of her to expect you to put your life on hold. Astrid will never grow up unless you help her along."

"You're interfering again," she said with frustration. "You've raised two wonderful daughters, but Astrid is my child and it's my responsibility to make the parenting decisions."

Of course, she was right. He wasn't entitled to tread on Lilly's toes and behave like Astrid's father. But he missed being part of a family, having had only a few precious years with his wife and daughters before cancer cruelly snatched Carla from him. What he saw in Lilly was a chance to experience family life a second time around, a way to be happy again.

"I'm sorry," he said, touching the sleeve of her sweater. "This is new territory for me, getting close to another woman after losing Carla. But I sense something special between us and I guess I wanted to jump right in with both feet."

"I know how you feel. I'm fighting that temptation too, but Astrid is in a difficult place and I have to tread super carefully."

At that moment, he was glad of Lilly's caution, pulling him back from the brink of recklessness. Was he really considering becoming part of another family, risking messing it up all over again? Or worse still, losing another woman that he adored.

"Shall we forget about the kiss?" he asked with a sinking heart. "And pretend it never happened?"

"I don't think I'll ever forget it," she said, bringing her fingertips to her lips. "But we shouldn't let it happen again. There's too much at stake."

He nodded. Lilly was a perfect voice of reason in this situation. She needed to protect Astrid, and he needed to protect his heart.

"I like you a lot, Lilly," he said, adding with a laugh, "in case you hadn't noticed. But I'll do my best to back off and give us both space."

She smiled, opened the bedroom door, slipped though and clicked it closed behind her. David placed his forehead onto the wall beside him, shut his eyes and let out a long exhalation of breath. This might be the lowest he'd felt since Chloe's accident, but it was the only way forward.

He'd often heard it said that lightning never strikes the same place twice. David had assumed that his strike had come in the untimely death of his wife, but he'd been wrong, because a second strike had hit his daughter a few years later. He knew he had to be mindful. Why give lightning a third chance to take down someone he loved?

Lilly skirted around David in the kitchen, awkwardly avoiding his eye as she cleared away her and Astrid's breakfast dishes. It had been a quiet and uneventful night, which had put her mind at rest regarding their safety, but the tension had not lifted in the house. She and David were like clumsy teenagers, recoiling when they accidentally brushed past one another, too afraid to begin a conversation for fear of betraying their true emotions.

It was apparently left to Goldie to try to clear the air.

"What's going on here?" she said, putting her hands flat on the counter. "You two are skittering around each other like cats on a roof."

David glanced at Lilly.

"We're…um…working through some stuff," he said. "It's no big deal."

Goldie wasn't easily fooled. "It's clearly a very big deal from what I can see. I don't know what's happened and I don't want to pry but the attraction between you two has been bubbling ever since you met." She picked up her mug of coffee and backed out of the kitchen. "I'm no expert on love, but I've never met two people who have more chemistry than you guys."

Once she had left David and Lilly alone, the awkwardness intensified, neither wanting to be the first to speak. Goldie was definitely correct about the chemistry. Lilly couldn't explain how or why, but she experienced a whole range of strong emotions when she was with David, a mixture of security, safety, familiarity and attraction. The certain click that she had never felt with

Rylan was present with David, and it was almost impossible to resist. But only almost.

"How did you sleep?" he asked, obviously aiming for a light conversation.

"Great. Astrid didn't have a nightmare so that's progress."

"It's good news that Henderson doesn't seem to be able to pinpoint us this time around. Hopefully, he'll continue to scope out the area using one of his aliases and get himself arrested so you can go home within a couple of days."

She smiled to hide a sudden and strange sense of dismay. A return to normalcy would be fantastic but it would mean losing David in her life and, despite having chosen that path willingly, it still hurt.

"Yeah," she said. "That would be best for everyone."

"What would be best for everyone?" Astrid said, coming into the room with an iPad in her hand.

Lilly crossed her arms and huffed. "It might be a good idea to stop listening to other people's conversations, Astrid. You could hear something that you didn't want to know."

"Whatever." Astrid sat on a stool at the kitchen bar and put the iPad on the counter. "I need to speak to you, Mom, about an email I got from Dad this morning."

Lilly shot her eyes to David's. "Did you say she could go online and check her messages?"

He nodded. "Yeah. It's one of our untraceable devices that allows incoming messages but blocks outgoing ones. It's totally safe."

"I'd rather have my own iPad back," Astrid said sulkily. "It's not fair."

"We talked about this already," David said patiently.

"Your devices are confiscated while you're in protective custody. It's vital for your safety."

Astrid made a guttural noise of disapproval and Lilly knew that an argument was brewing.

"What does your father say?" she asked, gearing herself up for the certain conflict that would follow. "This is the first time he's emailed you in a while, isn't it?"

"He says he'd like to come to visit for my birthday." Astrid was beyond excited. "That's great, right?"

Lilly was immediately suspicious. Rylan rarely made any effort unless there was a reward in it for him.

"How will he get to Oakmont?" she asked. "Does he give any details?"

"He says he'd like to book a flight but he's a little short on cash."

The look that passed between Lilly and David let her know that her fears were shared, and she was thankful for the silent support.

"He wondered if we could transfer some money to him," Astrid continued. "And he can make some definite plans."

Lilly really didn't want to ask the question, but knew she must. "How much does he want?"

"Two thousand dollars."

David obviously could stay silent no longer. "What? A round trip flight from California to Pennsylvania can't be more than a few hundred dollars. Why does he need two thousand?"

"I don't think it's any of your business how much money he needs," Astrid retorted. "He might need a car rental and hotels, and he probably wants to buy me a present too." She turned to her mother. "Can we send him the money?"

At that moment, Lilly hated Rylan for putting her in this position, for using Astrid to emotionally blackmail her into transferring money that would no doubt be spent on his extravagant vacation in Florida.

"I'm sorry, honey," she said. "I don't have that kind of money to spare."

Astrid smiled. "I already thought of this. Grandma and Grandpa have savings. We could ask them for a loan."

There was no way on this earth that Lilly would ask her parents to fund Rylan's vacation. "No, that's not fair to your grandparents. If your dad wants to come visit, he'll have to find the money himself."

"But if we don't send him the money, he won't come." Astrid's voice was rising higher and higher. "And I really want him to be here for my sixteenth birthday."

Lilly tried to be diplomatic. "Your father hasn't contributed financially to your upbringing since you were born. I don't think it's unreasonable to expect him to pay his own way to visit his daughter on her sixteenth birthday."

"You don't want him to be there for my birthday," Astrid challenged. "You probably want David there instead, and Dad would just make it awkward for you."

"This has nothing to do with me and David," Lilly said. "Please don't try and put the blame for your father's inadequacies on either of us."

Astrid knitted her eyebrows together. "What? You think Dad is inadequate?"

Lilly's skills of diplomacy were being stretched to the limit. "I think he could've tried harder to be a good father. There are too many times when he's let you down and he should own up to that."

"He just needs a little money to help him out," Astrid said, ignoring her mother's concerns. "Why do you have to be so mean?"

Lilly placed two fingertips lightly on her forehead, closed her eyes and sighed. She didn't want to fight with Astrid, not when her heart already hurt from trying to distance herself from David. There was no gas left in the tank.

As if sensing her pain, David stepped into the conversation.

"Astrid, your mother is the least mean person I know. She's kind and caring and beautiful, both inside and out. She's made a lot of sacrifices for your happiness, and she has every right to expect your father to step up and finance his own trip."

Astrid stared at him, lips pinched. "You've never even met my dad, so you have no idea what kind of a person he is."

"I can make a pretty good guess," he said. "He's always too busy to call or come to Oakmont, he has no idea what grades you get, he forgets your birthday, doesn't call at Christmas and hasn't once asked you to visit his home in California. Am I close?"

Astrid didn't respond for a while, looking as though she had been slapped. She clearly couldn't refute a single one of David's claims and Lilly didn't intervene to soften the blow. It was about time the truth was told.

"My dad isn't a deadbeat," Astrid said finally. "You only hate him because you're in love with my mom."

"I don't hate your father," David said. "And me being in love with your mom has nothing to do with your situation."

Lilly gasped a little. Did David just admit to being in love with her? Or was it a simple slip of the tongue?

"Mom and me are happy as we are," Astrid said. "We don't need you in our lives, so please stop trying to control me."

Lilly felt the need to diffuse the tension. "David's not trying to control you, honey. He's trying to help you face reality."

"He wants to steal Dad's place in our family," Astrid said, picking up the iPad and heading for the door. "Why can't you see it?"

Lilly's patience finally snapped. "Your dad doesn't have a place in our family, Astrid, so how could David steal it? Your father gave up his place voluntarily."

Astrid stopped and turned, so slowly that Lilly had plenty of time to prepare for the rage.

"He loves me!" she shouted out. "And he only wants a little money to come visit, except you're too cheap to help him."

David held out a hand. "I think it's time to give back the iPad," he said. "I don't want you reading emails from your father while we're in the safe house. It makes you anxious, and we need you to be calm right now."

Astrid walked a few steps across the kitchen tiles and slapped the device on David's flat palm.

"You're not cool," she muttered. "You're a tyrant."

"You remind me so much of Chloe," he said as she stalked away. "She was just like you a few years ago."

Astrid stopped in the doorway and made an attempt to stare him down. "You messed up your daughter's life, and now you want to mess up my life too."

"Astrid!" Lilly said. "That was a really unkind thing to say."

"It's okay, Lilly," David said lightly. "I'm learning to come to terms with what happened, and Astrid has helped me a lot, even when she's trying to hurt me." He smiled at her. "You're a really smart kid, and I hope we can be friends one day soon."

Astrid let out a low, guttural growl and flounced from the room. "We will never be friends," she said as she stomped up the stairs. "Ever."

David raised his eyebrows at Lilly. "Well, that sure told me, huh?"

Lilly was so grateful to David for intervening and backing her up, for being a solid and dependable force in dealing with Astrid. But there were consequences to her siding with David. Astrid was clearly struggling to cope with her father's unreliability and had built up a powerful fantasy in which Rylan was the good guy, the poor victimized parent being prevented from paying her a visit. And Astrid wouldn't listen to the truth.

"I should go after her," Lilly said. "Thank you for helping."

"It's my pleasure," he replied. "Teenage tantrums are my specialty." His expression changed to one of sadness. "It's one of the joys of family life, right?"

He held her gaze for longer than necessary and Lilly was reminded of Goldie's comment about her and David's chemistry. There was definitely something crackling through the air, an atmosphere impossible to touch, but easy to sense.

Lilly was the first to look away, her stomach awash with butterflies from the lingering gaze.

"I gotta go." She turned and fled the kitchen, deciding that the best way forward was to pretend that their simmering attraction simply didn't exist.

* * *

David was carrying out his checks on the doors and windows of the safe house when Goldie took him to one side in the hallway.

"Green Fingers Florist confirmed that they received a request for flowers to be delivered to Lilly Olsen," she said. "It was a telephone order from someone using a credit card that was later reported as stolen, and the man claimed that he wasn't sure of the exact house. He only had a street address and asked them to knock on all the doors to find the right one."

"He must've been watching from a distance," David said. "Waiting to see which house opened up. He must know that the street is unoccupied apart from us. Thankfully, I made sure to emerge from behind the house next door."

"We're keeping all the drapes and blinds closed and staying out of sight," Goldie said. "And the car is in the garage, so he won't be able to identify where we are."

"We'll have to implement a ban on turning on the lights at night," he said. "I know it's extreme but it's the only way. Did you pick up any more extra transmission signals?"

"Yeah, I did," she confirmed. "A little longer this time and it disappeared as I tried to get a lock on it."

He leaned against the wall and rubbed his eyes. "This is driving me crazy. We need to do another sweep of the house to be sure we're not bugged."

"I'll start on it right away." She touched his arm. "You look tired. This thing with Lilly has really got to you, hasn't it?"

His gut hadn't stopped churning all day. "I don't know

what to do. How can I feel this way about a woman after only knowing her a few days?"

Goldie shrugged. "I don't know how love works, but I guess your heart leads the way."

"That's true," he agreed. "But Lilly's heart is telling her that Astrid needs her time and attention right now."

"I can see why. Astrid has been really difficult to manage in the last day or two."

"I've also been thinking a lot about Carla recently," he said. "After she died, I never thought I'd love another woman."

"And now you're falling in love with Lilly, and you're scared you might lose her too?"

"It's a very real possibility," he said. "She's being hunted by one of the most wanted criminals in America." He rubbed his bristly chin. "I can't stop thinking about the ways she could get hurt. How do I make it stop, Goldie?"

"You keep a clear head and continue to do your job, making sure that Lilly and Astrid are both safe." She rested a reassuring hand on his shoulder. "And when your feelings and worries for Lilly are too heavy to bear, you give it up to God. Let Him take the strain."

"For someone who claims not to believe in love," he said with a smile, "you sure know how to give good advice when it comes to romance."

"Perhaps I missed my true calling as an advice columnist," she said. "What do you think?"

He laughed. "That's a terrible idea, but I'd love to see it happen."

Beneath their laughter, alarm bells rang. Literally.

"It's a red alert," David said, pulling the pager from

his belt. "Henderson's here. Secure Lilly and Astrid in their room and let's go take him down."

Goldie was gone in an instant and David raced down the stairs, dialing the number of the agents in the house across the street as he went.

"What have we got?" he asked when a voice answered. "Do we need backup?"

"Military backup has already been requested," came the reply. "We're in real trouble here, Agent McQueen."

"Military backup? What's going on?"

"Take a look out the window."

David parted the drapes in the living room, peering through to the end of the street where a vehicle was just rounding the corner. It was large and slow, turning on eight enormous wheels.

"What on earth is that?" he said to himself in amazement and horror, watching it lumber down the street, heading their way.

Goldie had obviously heard his open question as she came running down the stairs, closely followed by Lilly and Astrid.

"It's a Stryker," she said, her face drained of color. "A military-issued armored combat vehicle equipped with a machine gun and grenade launcher. Henderson must've stolen it from an Army base."

With Goldie's military background, she was the best person to assess the most appropriate course of action. "How do you suggest we fight something like this?" he asked.

Her reply was chilling. "We can't fight this. We have to run."

EIGHT

The huge green vehicle was like a tank on wheels instead of treads, heavy-duty and with a small turret on the top where the barrel of a gun was clearly visible. David knew that his bullets would offer no defense against its metal armor. The agent across the street was right—they were in real trouble.

"He still might not know our exact house," David said, clinging to a thread of hope.

Astrid gasped, her hands flying to her face. "I opened my bedroom window to let in some air. And I never closed it."

"That's all the evidence he needs." David hustled everyone into the kitchen. "Let's go."

As they ran, a torrent of bullets hit the living room window, shattering the glass and peppering the wall. In a split second, everyone dropped to the floor.

"Get out!" he shouted, crawling to open the back door, beckoning Astrid forward. "We'll find you a place to hide until backup arrives."

But Astrid was too afraid to move, curled up on the tiles with laced fingers on top of her bowed head. And the machine gunfire kept coming, sending pieces of plaster falling from the wall where the bullets were threatening to break through. The noise alone was enough to terrify anyone.

"Go on," Lilly urged, pulling Astrid's sleeve. "I'll be right behind you."

Astrid cried out in fear. "But he's outside. It's safer inside."

David scooted over to her just as there was a break in gunfire and he was able to hear the return fire from the agents across the street. The distraction could buy them some time to escape unnoticed.

"It might feel safer indoors, Astrid," he said, "but we're trapped. There's a grenade launcher on that vehicle and if the house collapses, we'll be underneath it." He took her hands from her head. "Take a look outside. There are no walls to fall on us and there's so much space to find somewhere better to hide."

Astrid lifted her head hesitantly and gazed toward the open door. "And we won't die?"

"We won't die," he said. "I promise that I won't let anything bad happen to you or your mom. You need to trust me on that."

"Okay." She began to crawl through the door, toward Goldie, who was already crouched on the patio, keeping watch. "You'll keep us safe." She appeared to be talking herself round, strengthening her mind. "I trust you."

Lilly followed in Astrid's path out into the open, where the machine gunfire broke through the eerie silence in the yard. David scanned the area in all directions, scouting for hiding places.

Shepherding everyone to the end of the lawn, he pointed to the high fence that ran along the back of the property. It was the best route to take them far away from Henderson's bullets, and it would lead them to the next block.

"We can all climb this, right?" he asked, looking down at Astrid's bare feet. In her haste, she'd forgotten to slip on some shoes. "I'll help." He made a steady platform with laced fingers. "Goldie, you go first and check the ground for hazards. I'll send Astrid over after you."

Before Goldie could place her foot on his hands, a huge explosion ripped through the air, creating a wind that blew across their faces and caused Astrid to scream. The whole house shook violently and the kitchen window crumpled, crashing from its frame to land on the patio outside.

"Grenade!" Goldie shouted. "The next one might be closer. There's no time to waste." She grabbed Astrid's hand and ran to the waist-high brick wall that lined both sides of the lawn. "Jump into next door's yard."

David took Lilly's hand and dragged her along with him, vaulting the property divider just in time to shield themselves from the next blast. The second grenade tore through the kitchen of their safe house, blowing out the entire back wall and taking out the wooden fence at the end of the yard. If they'd still been standing there, they'd probably be dealing with serious injuries by now.

"We need to keep going," David said, keeping hold of Lilly's hand and running across the lawn of the unoccupied house. "Let's head for the street and try to make it to the undercover agents' house. We need a car."

He vaulted the next wall, helping Lilly over and checking on Astrid. The teenager smiled weakly and he placed a comforting hand on her shoulder.

"You're doing great," he said. "I'm proud of you."

Astrid's gaze slid past his face to a point behind and

she opened her mouth to scream. Yet no sound came. She seemed to be frozen in horror.

David snapped his head to the right, seeing the armored vehicle come into view on a lawn about three houses away. Henderson had found a weak point to access the backyards and he was coming at them from another angle, determined to flush them out. The eight huge wheels of the military vehicle were easily able to crush the low boundary walls that divided the yards and he rode over them as if they were pebbles, crushing them beneath the black rubber tires.

"Run to the street," David yelled. "Stay together."

Goldie led the way, racing along the path at the side of the house, holding tight to Astrid. They emerged onto the street, deserted except for the undercover agents who had been stationed in the house opposite. The two men were on the sidewalk, guns in hand, anxiously speaking into their radios, obviously relaying the urgency of the situation to their superiors.

"We need to get out of here," David yelled to them. "Where's your vehicle?"

One of the agents pointed to the open garage of their house, where a van was peppered with bullet holes.

"Henderson shot it up and destroyed the engine as soon as I opened the door," he said. "I managed to get out of the way just in time."

This was not the news David wanted to hear as it took away their only means of escape. Outside their destroyed safe house was his SUV, hit by a grenade through the garage door. It had subsequently rolled down the driveway and was now a twisted mess of metal, smoldering and leaking fuel.

"A SWAT team is two minutes away," the agent said. "Where is Henderson now?"

"He's there!" Astrid screamed, pointing to the end of the street, where the armored vehicle was turning the corner, having doubled back on itself. "He's coming for us."

David turned in every direction. Where should he go? How could he safeguard the lives of Lilly and her daughter? They had no vehicle and were sitting ducks inside these empty houses. He was all out of ideas.

As he took a second or two to pray, someone tugged on his sleeve. It was Astrid.

"Look," she said, gesticulating to the street where a steady stream of gas was trickling from the car wreck on the driveway. "That's really flammable, right? Will we explode?"

Her words triggered an idea. "Astrid, you're a genius!" he exclaimed. "Stay with Goldie and your mom out of sight while I deal with Henderson."

He pointed to the house, took Astrid's hand and joined it to her mother's, before pushing them away from the scene.

"Help me shove this wreck from the driveway," he said to the undercover agents, watching Goldie lead Lilly and Astrid behind the agents' house, taking them out of Henderson's line of sight. "I want it bang in the middle of the street."

The three men used their shoulders to push the vehicle from its position and it rolled easily along the driveway. The machine gunfire started up as Henderson neared and the men used the car as a shield, crouching behind it while they steered it into the street.

"Go!" he yelled to the agents above the gunfire,

watching the wreck pick up speed, leaving a trickle of gasoline in its wake. "Take cover."

He ran toward the undercover house, pulling his gun and firing repeatedly at the ground, waiting for one of the bullets to create the necessary spark. The fourth bullet was the charm and the line of gasoline ignited, sending the car up in a whoosh of flames. The ball of fire picked up more speed as it approached the armored vehicle, finally slamming into it hard and halting in its tracks.

David smiled. There was no way forward for Henderson now, except to exit his vehicle. And so he waited. And waited. A military helicopter appeared overhead, flying low over the scene, a loud hailer ordering Henderson out into the open.

The fire in the SUV was becoming intense, creating a wall of heat that prevented David from going near. He peered through the flames, looking for signs of movement, but Henderson was making no attempt to escape. Maybe he'd passed out inside, overcome by the smoke.

The SWAT team screamed into view, closely followed by an Army combat vehicle and fire truck with lights flashing and sirens blaring. Surely this was the end for Henderson. He was surrounded by all manner of weaponry, both on the ground and in the air.

Checking behind him to ensure that Lilly and Astrid were safely shielded from any last-ditch fight back, David's hope increased as the firefighters doused the flames with water, while being protected by the armed SWAT team and a group of soldiers. Henderson was repeatedly ordered from the vehicle by the hovering helicopter, told to emerge with hands in the air.

Still no movement came.

Finally, one of the SWAT team members clambered

on top of the vehicle and opened the hatch, pointing his weapon and shouting out a warning.

"I think we got him," David yelled to Lilly, punching the air with relief. "We finally got him."

"No, sir, we don't," the SWAT officer called out. "It's empty."

David was disbelieving. "It can't be empty. Check again."

"I'm sorry, sir, but he's gone."

Lilly washed her face and patted it dry, careful not to drag the towel across her puffy and tender eyes. This situation was becoming intolerable and the fear in her gut had settled into a dull and constant throb. When David had first informed her of the need to enter witness protection, she had had no idea it would be this terrifying. She'd been putting on a brave face for Astrid's sake, but it was beginning to crack under the strain of constant attacks.

There was a soft knock on the door, a gentle voice calling her name. She took a deep breath, checked her reflection and opened up. David stood in the hallway of this remote and peaceful cabin in a beautiful wooded area outside the city.

"Astrid is worried about you," he said. "I offered to come see how you're doing."

"I'm okay." Her voice wobbled, forcing her to repeat her words. "I'm okay."

"You're clearly not okay," he said. "You look like you just cried a river."

Mention of her tears brought more of them forward and she used the towel to dab the corners of her eyes.

"How did Henderson get away again?" she asked. She had been euphoric at the expectation of his capture, and the bitter disappointment of his escape had been a gut punch. "I really thought this might be over."

"Me too." His face showed as much tension as she felt. "He stole the Stryker from an Army base while dressed as a solider, and he later modified it by blasting a hole in the base with explosives. He must've slipped underneath the vehicle and blended in with the Army unit to escape. I just didn't have my eyes peeled in the hive of activity. Next time we'll get him."

"Will we?" Wasn't that what they'd believed before and each time Henderson managed to flee from justice? "Or will I be stuck in witness protection with my daughter for weeks or months or years? I don't know how much more I can take, David. He keeps finding us and we have no idea how. How do we know we're safer here than the places we've already been?"

"This cabin is really off the beaten track," he said. "And it's location is only known by Goldie and me. We decided to go totally off-grid this time. Even if there is a mole inside the FBI, he won't be able to pass any location information to Henderson because he won't have it."

Far from reassuring Lilly, this made her even more fearful. "That means we're all alone here in the woods, far away from any help." She started to gasp for air, panic setting in. "We could all die here."

"Calm down." He took steady, soothing breaths. "Breathe along with me. In and out."

Lilly watched his chest rise and fall beneath his shirt and matched the rhythm, forcing herself to quell the fear. She didn't want to spiral out of control.

"I don't want Astrid to see me like this," she said when she was able to speak again. "Can you tell her that I have an upset stomach or something? I should be with her right now, but I can't offer her any support." A sob caught in her throat. "I feel like such a failure. My daughter needs me to be strong, but I'm here in the bathroom crying like a baby. I'm useless."

"You're not useless, Lilly."

He gripped both her shoulders and she almost fell into his chest, resting her forehead against the white cotton of his shirt. He was a haven of safety in the chaos of a storm and she was too weak to put an emotional distance between them.

David wound his fingers through her hair at the base of her neck and rested his hand there, warm and weighty on her nape.

"Astrid is fine," he whispered. "Goldie is great with her and they're talking in the living room about what's happened. She's in good hands."

"That's reassuring." Lilly was relieved. "At least somebody is being strong for her."

"Listen to me, Lilly." David pulled away to hold her face in his hands. "I know exactly how it feels to believe that you've failed at parenting. I've felt like a failure for the last five years, but I've just started to accept that parents can't be perfect all the time. We're human too, and we make mistakes, we get mad, we cry, we hurt and we regret things." He smiled. "Parenting is messy."

"I'm so worried," Lilly said. "What if I'm not leading Astrid along the right path? What if I'm subjecting her to experiences that will have a terrible effect on her later on? What if she ends up going off the rails and making bad choices…?" She trailed off, realizing that she was drawing parallels with David's situation.

He knew what she was referring to. "You're worried she'll end up like Chloe, right?"

Lilly nodded, too shamefaced to speak. She was concerned that Astrid had a similar character to Chloe, hotheaded and defiant, liable to rebel and defy authority.

"I learned something really important recently," David said, continuing to hold her head in his hands. "Bad experiences don't always lead to bad things. Sometimes they help us learn and grow, to make us better people. Chloe never wanted to be a doctor, but I was too stubborn to see it, and I've been judging her based on my own high expectations. She's so much happier stocking shelves in a grocery store than she would be as a doctor."

Lilly was confused. "Do you think her accident was a good thing?"

"Not a good thing exactly," he replied. "But God worked it to her advantage. He turned something incredibly tragic into something very positive, and her life is great."

Lilly wanted to have as much faith as David did, but it seemed that God was so far away at that precise moment.

"I wish I could believe everything will work out for the best, but I don't feel it inside. I keep thinking of all the things that can go wrong." Another sob caught her off guard. "I couldn't bear to see Astrid suffer." She stared into his eyes. "How did you cope when Chloe was suffering? How did you stand it?"

"I didn't have a choice," he said. "I'd have done anything to switch places with her when she was in the hospital bed, but she had to learn to be strong on her own. It's natural to want to protect your kids from pain but it's unrealistic. They have to be independent."

This was a surprising change in David's attitude. "You always say that parents should be strict with children and stop them being too independent."

"Yeah, well I kind of changed my mind, and I want to apologize for being so hard on you, Lilly. You're a strong mother and you're doing a great job with Astrid. You give her enough freedom to make her own choices and her own mistakes. You're letting her grow up."

This praise was enough to bring back the tears. "I'm sorry." She wiped her sore eyes. "Everything is making me cry right now, even compliments."

He drew her into an embrace. "That's okay. Your body will run out of water eventually."

She laughed. "And I'll end up like a dried old prune."

"But you'd still be beautiful."

"Thank you," she said. "You always know how to make me feel better."

"Okay." He withdrew from her, becoming more businesslike. "It's getting late. You and Astrid need to get some rest. Come join us in the living room when you're ready and we'll get you settled into your room for the night."

He turned to leave, but she reached out and grabbed his hand, driven by a need to know how he felt.

"Do you really sense something special between us?"

Bringing her fingers to his lips, he kissed them softly. "I've haven't felt this way since I met my wife twenty-seven years ago. But I respect your boundaries and I'll keep my distance."

He released her hand and closed the door, leaving her alone with her relentless tears.

David cleared away the leftovers of their meager meal, rustled up from hastily bought supplies on their way to the cabin. He had insisted that this next safe house be a total secret, even from his superiors, putting control in his hands alone. Henderson had been able to decipher their location three times and the only explanation was a traitor in the ranks. David was taking absolutely no chances this time around.

Goldie entered the kitchen. "Lilly and Astrid are unpacking in their room," she said. "Astrid says a cosmetics purse is missing. She's worked herself up into a state about it because she says it's really important."

David pointed to a backpack in the corner, which he had filled with stray items from the previous safe house. The ferocious grenade attack had rendered the building unsafe and their belongings had been strewn into all corners, but he'd done his best to ensure that Lilly and Astrid lost nothing. Henderson shouldn't be allowed to deprive them of one single thing.

"Astrid's purse might be in there," he said. "Get her to check."

Goldie hesitated in the doorway. "You look dog-tired."

He stopped loading the dishwasher and leaned against the counter. "I think this might be the most difficult assignment I've ever worked. Not only are we being sold out by someone on the inside, but I have to battle with my feelings for Lilly and tread on eggshells with Astrid." He ran a hand down his beard. "But I guess we're all feeling the strain, not just me."

Goldie sat at the kitchen table. "I'm still investigating who our mole might be, but there are no leads. All the agents working our case seem to be squeaky-clean." She sighed deeply. "It's kind of a relief in one way, but it would help to know there was a bad apple somewhere."

He sat at the table opposite her. "This case has got me totally paranoid, especially about bugging devices and tracking signals."

"We're clean, David. I checked three times."

Goldie smiled when his face clearly showed skepticism. "We're clean," she said emphatically. "I made sure to choose a cabin in a black spot. There's no Wi-Fi, no cell phone signal, no GPS and no way of tracking us here."

"What about Henderson? Have any of his aliases given us a new lead?"

"I'm afraid he's disappeared. We've got all our trusted agents trying to trace him, but he's a master of disguise and he's vanished into thin air."

"So we're totally in the dark here in more ways than one."

"Yes, we are," she said. "But I won't rest until we get a good lead. I'm determined to catch this guy."

"Thank you, Goldie."

She rose from the table. "I'm glad to be able to help. I only wish I could solve your love problems so easily."

"So do I," he said, remembering the sorrow on Lilly's face in the bathroom, and how his heart heaved for her. "I sure could use some guidance."

Lilly and Astrid's voices carried down the hallway, Astrid's loud and insistent, Lilly's gentle and appeasing.

"I need it, Mom," Astrid said, coming into the kitchen. "I know you think I'm being stupid but it's really important to me."

"You're beautiful as you are, honey," Lilly said. "You don't need the makeup."

"Yes, I do." Astrid looked at Goldie hopefully. "Did you find my cosmetics purse?"

"Check the backpack in the corner," Goldie replied. "It might be in there."

David looked up at Lilly. Her hair was scraped back into a ponytail, highlighting the slenderness of her face, but her forehead was furrowed as she watched Astrid search in the backpack for her purse. David wanted to go to her and gather her in his arms, to whisper that he would take care of her and make everything right again. But it would be the wrong thing to do for both of them.

She caught his eye and smiled faintly. "Astrid thinks she can't live without lipstick and eye shadow," she said. "I just can't seem to persuade her otherwise."

Astrid stood triumphantly. "Got it," she said, holding a gold purse aloft. "It's here."

"Your mom's right, Astrid," David said. "Your natural face is beautiful and I'm sure Noah would agree too. That's your boyfriend's name, right? The kid with the curly hair?"

She turned sheepish, staring down at the floor. "Noah likes me for who I am. I really miss him."

"You'll see him soon enough," David said. "Just hold on a little while longer."

"You think it'll be soon?" There was hope in Astrid's voice. "I want to go home so much."

David walked over to her. "I'll do everything in my power to get you home in plenty of time for your sixteenth birthday in a week's time. And if that's not possible, I'll throw you a party myself, okay?"

She smiled. "Thank you."

He waited for her to mention her father and his possible birthday visit, but she remained silent, so he placed a hand on her shoulder. "I also want to thank you for noticing the leaking fuel from the car and giving me the idea of setting it on fire. You saved us today, Astrid. Well done."

She grinned and looked at her mother. "Did you know I came up with a genius plan today, Mom?"

"No, I didn't." Lilly hugged Astrid from behind, kissing the back of her head. "You have all the best ideas."

"I'm also really tired," she said, letting her head fall onto her mother's shoulders. "It's past eleven."

"Let's turn in for the night," Lilly said, leading Astrid to the door. "It's so peaceful here. You'll sleep like a log."

Astrid tucked her purse into her armpit, rubbed her eyes. "This is a safer place than the last one, isn't it?" she asked, sounding as though she were trying to convince herself. "He'll never find us here."

David swallowed his fears and reassured her. "We're completely cut off from the world," he said. "No signals can get in or out. We're untraceable."

Lilly smiled. "There are worse places to be cut off, I guess."

With its picturesque views, endless greenery and forest surroundings, this cabin was a haven of tranquility, and David hoped that Lilly would be able to relax enough to enjoy it. She sure needed it.

"Sleep well, you two," he said. "Goldie and I will take turns on lookout shift, so someone will be watching over you through the night."

"That's what God does too, right?" Astrid said. "He never sleeps."

David wasn't sure if she was teasing him, but he could detect no sarcasm in her voice. She appeared to be asking a genuine question.

"That's exactly right, Astrid," he said. "God will be watching over you too."

"I'm sorry I made fun of you when you talked about your faith." She avoided his eye. "I feel bad about it."

He was pleasantly shocked to hear those words. "It

takes guts to apologize when you've done wrong," he said. "I appreciate it."

Astrid took hold of her mother's hand and walked from the room, looking to be so much younger than her fifteen years without the black lipstick and eye shadow. And she was revealing a vulnerable side that activated his paternal streak.

In the hallway, Lilly glanced back, silently mouthed the words *thank you* and gave him a thumbs-up.

David smiled in response and watched them head off to their room, hand in hand. He realized that he was growing as attached to Astrid as he was to her mother. Astrid was rebellious, difficult and rude, but she was a good kid underneath.

Her new, more mature attitude might just soften Lilly's resistance to a possible romantic relationship. Could David dare to hope that he had a second chance at love? Would his daughters be happy for him if another woman entered his life or would they resent his attention being directed away from them?

He shook his head, rousing himself from the ridiculous fantasy.

"It's not gonna happen, David," he told himself. "Never in a million years."

Lilly tucked Astrid into bed just like she used to when she was a toddler, pulling the sheet taut around her body.

"Too tight, Mom." Astrid laughed. "I can't breathe."

She loosened the sheet. "You used to like the feeling of being tucked in nice and tight when you were small." Lilly picked up White Bear from the shelf overhead and handed it to her daughter. "You always looked so peaceful when you slept."

Astrid pushed the cuddly toy away. "I don't think I want White Bear tonight. In fact, I'm not sure I need him anymore."

"Really?" Lilly felt her eyes widening. "But you love White Bear. He always sleeps with you."

"I'm almost sixteen. It's time to put away childish things—isn't that what you sometimes say?"

She was amazed that Astrid actually remembered her occasional words of advice, especially the ones taken from Scripture.

"Well, okay then," Lilly said, placing White Bear back on the shelf. "I'll just leave him there in case you need him in the night."

"I won't need him."

Lilly pushed Astrid's hair from her forehead. "You seem a little different tonight. What happened?"

Astrid thought carefully before replying. "David put his life on the line trying to protect us today. He could've gotten himself killed but he didn't give up." She chewed her lip. "And Dad won't even come visit for my birthday unless we pay him. What I saw David do today really made me think about things. I had an epi-phoney or whatever you call it."

"I think you mean an epiphany, honey."

"Yeah, I had one of those. I want to be a better person, Mom. I really do."

"You're already a great person," Lilly said, stroking her cheek. "But there's always room for improvement."

"I've been really mean to David and said bad things, and he doesn't deserve it." She rubbed the cotton bedsheet between her thumb and forefinger. "He's a nice man."

"I think so too."

"I know you like each other a lot." She smiled. "A whole lot."

"We respect each other," Lilly said diplomatically. "And we're friends."

"Friends who kiss each other are more than friends, Mom."

They both burst into laughter. It felt good to be light-hearted with Astrid again. She had seemed to be so distant lately and now there was a glimmer of light at the end of the tunnel.

"Yes, David became more than a friend," Lilly said. "I didn't mean for it to happen, but it did."

"You can't help who you fall in love with," Astrid said. "And I think you fell in love with him."

Lilly wondered if this conversation had gone too far. "Perhaps I did, but that's not any of your business, missy."

Astrid smiled. "I just wanted to say that I won't cause any more problems for you." She pulled a serious face, put on a deep voice. "You have my blessing."

This prompted a real belly laugh from Lilly. "I have your blessing? That's hilarious."

"I know," Astrid said with a giggle. "Who knew that I was both smart *and* funny?"

"I did," she said, kissing her daughter's forehead. "But my and David's relationship is more complicated than you think."

"It is?"

Lilly wanted to be honest with Astrid but also wanted to shield her from adult worries and fears. She tried to be careful with her response.

"I loved your father once," she said. "I really did."

Astrid seemed to read her mind. "And he let us down, didn't he?"

"Yes, he did, so I need to be absolutely certain of David's intentions before I trust him."

"Mom," Astrid said, propping herself up onto her elbows. "David would die for you." She placed the back of her hand onto her forehead, theatrically. "He's like a movie star hero rushing to save the heroine, who's stuck on a rock in the middle of a flood or something."

Lilly let out another laugh. "That's a very creative fantasy."

"It's not a fantasy. It's what David does for us every day, right?"

"Yeah," Lilly admitted. "He's one of the good guys."

"So why are you worried about his intentions?"

It was time to bring this conversation to a close. Lilly stood up, smiling brightly.

"It's late. Sleep tight, honey. I'll be in the bed right across from yours, okay?"

"Okay, Mom. I'll stop asking hard questions. I love you."

"Love you too."

Lilly padded across the floorboards in her socks and went into the bathroom. Shutting the door, she contemplated the words she had just exchanged with Astrid, realizing that the most significant barrier to a relationship with David had now been removed. Could she bring herself to let go of her fears and trust him to be a better man and father figure than Rylan had ever been? No matter how decent David had shown himself to be, there was always a seed of doubt, a lingering worry that he might skip out on them when the tantrums and arguments were too overwhelming. Astrid could test anyone's patience.

The most sensible thing to do was to wait a little while, to be sure of making the correct decision. At fifteen years old, Astrid was unpredictable, prone to mood changes for the slightest of reasons, and her attitude tomorrow might be in stark opposition to the one she displayed tonight. She could easily return to her old habits of baiting David with her rudeness. Waiting was definitely sensible.

After all, there was no point in rushing into things without testing the water first.

NINE

David rolled the dice and moved his piece along the board. It had been many years since he'd sat at a table playing a game, feeling part of a family. And he liked it.

"Okay, listen up," Astrid said, picking up a card. "If you get this question right, you win the game. You ready, David?"

"As ready as I'll ever be," he said. "Shoot."

Astrid slid her eyes over to her mother. "No helping him, okay, Mom?" She inhaled a dramatic breath. "Who was the fortieth president of the United States of America?"

David already knew the answer to this one, but he pretended to struggle as he tapped his temple. "Now let me think."

Astrid was taking this quiz very seriously and shot Lilly and Goldie severe glances, warning them against lending assistance. She had found the game at the back of a cupboard and had persuaded everyone to play around the coffee table after dinner. On a wet and windy night, with the fire burning brightly in the hearth, the atmosphere in the cabin was cozy and comfortable. With no sign of Henderson having found them, David thought that their fortunes might have finally changed for the better.

"I think the answer is Ronald Reagan," he said.

Astrid dropped her shoulders in defeat. "Yeah, that's correct. You win. You're too smart for us."

"That's not fair," said Lilly playfully. "I was given all the hard questions. David got an easy ride with his simple ones."

"Yeah, you might be right," Astrid said, resetting the board. "His questions were kinda easy, so we should have a rematch." She smiled at him. "Perhaps you're not so smart after all."

He put a hand across his heart. "That's harsh. I won fair and square."

"Maybe we should pair up for the next round," Astrid suggested. "Mom, you go with Goldie and I'll go with Dad...I mean David." She blushed furiously. "Sorry, it was a slip of the tongue."

The room fell momentarily silent while Astrid busied herself with the pieces of the game, clearly mortified. In contrast, David felt honored that she would accidentally call him dad. It meant he had made a breakthrough.

"Don't worry about it, honey," Lilly said, obviously wanting to cover her daughter's embarrassment. "David sounds a lot like dad when you say it quickly, and we all mispronounce names sometimes. Do you remember when somebody called you Aspen by mistake?"

"Of course I do," Astrid said. "I actually preferred it. Astrid is a horrible name."

"Not this again," Lilly said, side-eyeing David for backup. "Astrid hates her name. She thinks it's awful."

At this, Goldie jumped into the conversation. "You're

kidding me. I'd love to be named Astrid. It's so beautiful."

"But Goldie is much nicer," Astrid said.

"Goldie is the short version of my real name," she said. "The longer version isn't so great."

Astrid thought for a few moments. "Is your name Goldilocks?"

The laughter that bounced around the room lifted David's spirits even higher. Now he truly did feel as though he were part of a loving family.

Goldie wiped the moisture from beneath her eyes. "My name is Marigold."

David's laughter wouldn't subside. "I prefer Goldilocks," he said. "It suits you."

Goldie gave Astrid a look of mock disapproval. "Now look what you started."

"Sorry," she said with a grimace. "I like the name Marigold too. It's nice." She didn't sound convinced. "Sort of."

"It's a super old-fashioned name," Goldie said. "So next time you find yourself wishing that you weren't called Astrid, just remember that you could be called Marigold instead."

Lilly reached for and squeezed David's hand beneath the table. He wasn't quite sure what her affections meant, but he didn't try to analyze the gesture. He simply enjoyed the sensation of her hand in his and squeezed back.

Goldie stood. "I'll take a rain check on the rematch. I'd like to go touch base with headquarters and get an update on the hunt for Henderson."

"There's no cell phone reception here," Astrid said. "We're in a black hole, remember?"

"I'll take a walk to the top of the hill," Goldie replied,

sinking her feet into her boots. "That's where you catch a signal."

"Take a raincoat," Astrid said. "It's wet out there, Goldilocks."

Goldie walked out into the hallway, shaking her head. "I guess I'd better get used to this."

"Don't go eating anybody's porridge," David called out. "And stay away from bears."

"That's a good one," Astrid said to him. "We could have fun with this."

David heard the front door open and close and the key being turned in the lock to make them secure. He then looked across at Lilly, who seemed so relaxed and content that he could almost imagine their previous arguments and bickering had never happened.

"This is nice, huh?" he said. "It makes a change from the last few days."

Lilly nodded in agreement. "Yes, it does. We all needed an evening like this to recharge." She slipped her hand from David's and began to clear away the board pieces. "I think it might be a little late for another game, so let's save it for tomorrow." She flashed him a smile. "I have a score to settle."

He smiled back at her, holding eye contact for a long while, as she tucked her hair behind her ears, her breath quickening.

"I'll go make some bedtime cocoa," Astrid said. "And leave you two to hold hands some more."

Lilly gave Astrid a sharp look that David assumed was meant to caution her against overstepping.

"I saw you holding hands under the table," Astrid said, ignoring her mother's warning. "And I think it's cute."

Barely a day had passed since Astrid had thrown a

tantrum at the thought of David taking her father's place, yet she seemed to have totally changed her tune. And he had no idea why.

The astute teenager was obviously able to read his thoughts. "Everything you said about my dad was true," she said quietly. "I didn't want to admit that he's a loser, but there's no point in pretending anymore. I need to stop making an effort for him because he doesn't deserve me."

Lilly once again reached for David's hand and he took it, sandwiching it between his own. They were a united front.

"What made you change your mind about me?" he asked.

"Yesterday, you told me you were proud of me and I realized that I've never once heard my dad say that. He's never shown an interest in me or taken the time to get to know me. He's never even sent me to my room when I'm acting up. You've done all of those things, so I guess you really do care about me. You're pretty cool for a norm."

He was shocked into silence for a few seconds. This was unexpected praise from a young woman who had seemed determined to oust him from her family at any cost.

"Thank you," he said, reaching across and patting her hand. "And you're pretty cool for a goth."

She rolled her eyes and he smiled. Some things never changed. "I'm not a goth anymore," she said. "I'm an indie kid now."

"Oh, right." He knitted his eyebrows in confusion. "Good for you. What's an indie kid?"

"Never mind. You wouldn't understand." She stood up. "I really enjoyed this evening. It was fun. I'll go make cocoa for everybody."

David watched her leave the room, turned to Lilly and said, "Who is that, and what did you do with the real Astrid?"

Lilly threw back her head and laughed. "I don't know what happened to her, but it's like she finally grew up."

David shifted himself closer to her on the couch, their knees touching, her hand sandwiched between his. In the kitchen, Lilly heard the kettle boiling, the clanking of cups and spoons. Astrid was actually being helpful.

"It's quite an amazing difference," David said. "I like this new Astrid a lot more than the old one."

Lilly lowered her voice. She didn't want to be over-heard. "I'm worried that the old Astrid might make a reappearance. In fact, I'm worried about a lot of things, but I'm trying to let them go."

"What else is worrying you?"

"I just…it's difficult to explain." She was tongue-tied. "I'm not very good at talking about my feelings like this."

"Try. I promise not to interrupt."

She took a steadying breath. "When I found out I was pregnant with Astrid, I imagined that my life would be wonderful. I thought that Rylan and I would get married and buy a house and maybe have some more kids later on." She stared into his eyes. "But it all went wrong because I totally misjudged him."

"I guess that must make it hard to trust another man," he said. "I understand."

"I really like you, David. My heart tells me that you're an honorable man, but my head keeps reminding me that Rylan ran away as soon as the going got tough."

"Not all men are the same," he said. "I can't imagine

why Rylan chose to walk away from his beautiful family, but that's his loss. Don't let it stop you from being happy again."

"Do you think that…?" She stopped, turned her head and blushed. Laying her emotions wide-open was hard. "Do you think that we could be happy together? I mean really happy?"

He squeezed her hand again. "Yes, I do, but I have worries just like you, Lilly. Losing my wife and almost losing my daughter has left its mark. Seeing you and Astrid together sometimes breaks my heart because it reminds me of what my daughters have lost. It reminds me that it could happen all over again."

Tears sprung into Lilly's eyes at the sight of David's vulnerability, while he shared his innermost fears.

"Looks like we're both afraid to take a chance, huh?" she said.

"I want to," he said. "I really do."

"If it helps at all, Astrid told me she gives us her blessing."

David laughed, loud and long. "That's good to know."

"Astrid might change her mind in a few days' time, so I'm not sure that her blessing carries any weight," Lilly said. "She has this amazing tendency to mess up all the good things in her life. It's almost as though she sabotages her own happiness before something bad happens to steal it away. Does that make sense?"

"Of course it makes sense. Astrid has been dealing with rejection from her father her whole life and that must've taken a toll. She has trust issues. You both have trust issues because of what Rylan has done. That's normal."

"Where do we go from here?" she asked, conscious of a flush remaining on her face. "I'm not sure what to do."

He placed both palms on her cheeks, holding her face gently, his thumbs rubbing the skin beneath her eyes, the parts that had been sore and puffy yesterday.

"You can trust me, Lilly," he said, leaning his head toward hers. "I give you my word that I won't hurt you or Astrid. I have no idea how this will work out in the end, but all I know is that you mean a lot to me."

"You mean a lot to me, too," she whispered.

When their mouths met, it was a moment of perfect calm, with the sound of rain splattering on the window behind them and the fire crackling in the room. Lilly closed her eyes and enjoyed the softness and warmth of David's lips on hers.

Yet her doubts refused to be pushed aside, taunting her with the possibility that her newfound happiness could be snuffed out in an instant. There was a good chance that Henderson would find them again and launch an even more audacious attack than before. Or Astrid could return to her old ways and decide to ruin her and David's developing, yet fragile, relationship.

In all likelihood, Lilly thought she would end up facing both scenarios.

David whistled a tune as he made coffee in the early morning light. Two nights had passed in the cabin without incident, and his mind was finally free of worry. It would appear that their plan to go off-grid had worked. They were untraceable.

"You're cheerful this morning," Goldie said, entering the kitchen and placing some pastries from the store on the table. "Does it have anything to do with Lilly by any chance?"

"Maybe." He decided to keep this feeling all to himself. "But I'm also happy about this place being so secure. We finally managed to outsmart Henderson."

"I don't want to spoil your mood but I just got some news from headquarters while I took a drive to the store."

"What?"

"The alarm to Lilly's home in Oakmont was triggered overnight, so it looks like Henderson broke in to search for her."

"Did the police respond?"

"They were there within seven minutes but he was gone."

Far from spoiling his mood, this information buoyed David up.

"This is great news," he said. "If Henderson is looking for Lilly in Oakmont, that means he has no idea where we are, right? And if he continues to target her home, it's only a matter of time before he's arrested."

Goldie poured herself a coffee from the filled pot. "Wow, nothing can dampen your high spirits this morning, huh? What has caused this joyfulness? Because I'd like some of it too, please."

He smiled. "Lilly and I are growing closer. It's not going to be plain sailing for either of us, but we had a good conversation last night and were totally honest with one another. Have you ever had one of those conversations where you make a strong connection?"

Goldie made a retching noise. "You know I don't like that kind of mushy stuff."

He laughed. "Maybe one day you'll change your mind."

"Never."

He poured coffee into a cup on the counter, almost dropping the pot when a scream rang through the cabin and Lilly came tearing down the hallway in her robe and slippers.

"Astrid's missing," she said, ashen-faced and clutching the door frame in the kitchen. "I think somebody took her."

David put down the pot and grabbed his gun from its holster. "Where did you last see her?"

"She went into the bathroom to take a shower, but after thirty minutes I got worried so I went inside and the water was still running but the window was open and…" She covered her mouth and sobbed. "She must've been pulled out the window." She grabbed at David's shirt. "You have to find her. Please."

"You stay with Goldie," he said. "I'll go into the woods and look. I'll organize a search party if I don't find her."

Lilly collapsed into a heap on the floor, head in her hands, weeping uncontrollably.

"I'll find her," he called, as he ran to the front door. "She can't have gotten far."

Flying through the door, he immediately began to shout Astrid's name, running up the hill toward the thick patch of trees that overlooked their secluded cabin. Keeping his gun at his side, he fought hard to stop himself imagining Astrid in the hands of Henderson and how she could be used as a bargaining chip to get to Lilly. This simply couldn't be happening. All windows had been secure on his morning checks, so how had Henderson gained access?

"Astrid!" he yelled into the quietness, disturbing a flock of birds in the trees. "Where are you? Call out to me if you can."

He waited and listened, his breath short and ragged from sprinting up the steep incline.

"I'm here." A voice traveled from the top of the hill. "I'm right here."

Astrid jogged toward him, wearing a sweat suit and sneakers and looking as though she didn't have a care in the world. He ran to meet her.

"Where were you?" he asked. "Your mom thought you'd been snatched out the bathroom window."

"I wanted to go for a jog," she said innocently. "I needed the fresh air and exercise."

He took a moment to regain his breath and gather his thoughts. Something didn't add up.

"You wanted to go for a jog?" he said. "So you decided to jump out the bathroom window without telling anybody?"

She avoided his eye. "Yeah. I thought Mom would say no, so I snuck out."

"I want you to tell me the truth, Astrid."

"I *am* telling the truth."

He felt the need to emphasize the importance of honesty. "Remember our code of conduct, Astrid. I trust you and you trust me, so we keep no secrets from each other, right? And we absolutely do not lie."

She finally looked him in the eye and he saw fear. "I didn't tell a lie."

Astrid's cosmetics purse was in her right hand, almost behind her back as if she were trying to shield it from view. "Where have you been?"

"I told you," she said defensively. "I went for a jog."

"With your makeup purse?"

"Yeah. I like to take it with me everywhere I go."

He fixed her with a steely eye. "Let me see inside."

"No."

"It wasn't a request, Astrid. It was an order. Let me see inside the purse."

She took a step away from him. "You have no right to pry into my things. You're a bully." Here was the old Astrid, rude and defiant as ever. "Leave me alone."

He heard a voice and glanced back to see Lilly running up the hill, closely followed by Goldie. Lilly had changed into jeans and a hooded sweatshirt, and her messy hair was flowing behind her. The look on her face was mixed—part anger, part relief.

"Astrid," she shouted. "Please tell me you didn't climb out that window of your own free will. I've been worried sick about you."

"I went for a jog, Mom," Astrid replied with a huff. "Why do you all have to make such a big deal of it?"

Lilly reached her daughter, breathless and sweating, and enveloped her in a hug before admonishing her.

"You've never jogged anywhere in your life. What are you hiding?"

David's fears intensified in his belly. He was pretty sure he knew exactly what Astrid was hiding, but she was refusing to cooperate.

"I think Astrid might be our mole," he said. "She's the reason Henderson keeps finding us."

Astrid was incredulous. "That's not true."

"Isn't it?" His eyes flicked to her purse. "Then you don't have a secret cell phone in your purse that you've been using the whole time you've been in protective custody?"

She turned pink, deciding to come clean. "I've hardly used it. I keep it switched off nearly all the time and I've literally only sent about six or seven instant messages to

Noah." Her voice faded under the horrified gaze of all three adults. "I never used it for emails or public posts on social media. It was just a few private messages. I figured they'd be safe because they're private."

"Oh, Astrid." Lilly ran a hand down her face. "How did you get this cell phone?"

"Noah secretly passed it to me through my bedroom window just before we left Oakmont to go to the safe house." Her bottom lip began to wobble. "He said I could use it to keep in touch with him while I was away. We didn't think it would be a big deal."

"You didn't think it would be a big deal?" David's voice echoed through the trees. "You placed us in danger repeatedly, and to make matters worse, you lied to me, Astrid. A few days ago, you promised me that you wouldn't contact anybody while we were in the safe house." He shook his head. He had totally misread the maturity of this young woman. "We have to leave immediately. Henderson will already be on his way here."

"But it's just one little Snapchat message to Noah," Astrid said. "I didn't even tell him where we are."

"All online messages can be tracked with geotagging," he said. "And the first person whose internet accounts Henderson will hack are Noah's. All it takes is one little message for him to discover our general location and then he just needs to stake out the area and look for ways to flush us out." He ushered her down the hill. "I'm so angry with you right now that I can't even look at you." He held out his palm. "Give me the phone."

"I'm sorry," she said, unzipping her purse and taking out the cell. "I honestly never realized it was me leading Henderson to us. I thought it was somebody inside the FBI, just like you said."

"You betrayed us." After everything he had been through with Chloe—the lies and deceit and arguments— he couldn't overlook the dishonesty. "I thought you had matured, but I was wrong." He took the cell and removed the battery. "This might be the worst thing you've ever done."

"Hey," Lilly said, pulling on his sleeve. "She knows she's messed up and she's sorry about it. Cut her some slack."

"She's been putting us in danger time and time again," he said. "You might be able to tolerate her lies but I can't."

Lilly and Astrid struggled to keep pace with him, while Goldie hung at the back, keeping watch.

"Don't be so hard on her," Lilly said. "She's a child."

David couldn't believe he was back here again, arguing about Astrid and her behavior. He'd known she would take a couple of steps back on her path to adulthood, but this went far beyond anything he could abide.

"She's not a toddler, Lilly," he said. "She's almost sixteen, and I clearly hold her to a higher standard than you do."

"Who do you think you are?" Lilly challenged as they approached the cabin. "You have no right to judge me for showing compassion to my daughter. I can't believe I ever allowed myself to feel something for you."

His heart heaved with pain and regret and a fear of losing Lilly's affections, but they were facing an imminent attack and Astrid's foolishness was the cause.

"Everybody get in the car," he yelled, noticing that storm clouds had gathered overhead. "Leave your belongings behind. I'll arrange to get them transferred to us later. It looks like heavy rain is coming so let's go now."

Astrid didn't argue. She climbed into the SUV, pulled on her belt and sat beside her mother, tears rolling down her face.

No matter how hard David tried to summon a spirit of forgiveness, it would not come. The only emotions he could feel at that moment were anger and disappointment. Astrid had let him down in the most terrible way, and he didn't think that his and Lilly's relationship could survive the betrayal.

Lilly gripped Astrid's hand as the SUV sped out of the woods, wipers moving fast to clear the rain as it lashed down from the darkened sky. She knew that Astrid deserved to be punished for her lies, but she first needed to be forgiven and Lilly was making a big attempt to be supportive rather than judgmental. David, however, was making the situation ten times worse with his refusal to even try to understand.

"Do you think you could slow down a little?" Lilly said, watching the fat raindrops bounce on the surface ahead. "The road is wet, so it could be dangerous."

David's face was stony in the driver's seat. "We need to move quickly. If Henderson was in Oakmont overnight, he could be here already. It's not that far away from us."

"She didn't understand that her private messages could be tracked," Lilly said, seeing Astrid's chin drop onto her chest. "She just wanted to stay in touch with her boyfriend like any teenager would. I know she's done a bad thing, but she realizes her mistake, and she's sorry."

David looked in the rearview mirror, resting his eyes on Astrid. "Are you sorry, Astrid?" he asked.

She refused to raise her head, but Lilly saw her jaw

clench as she sniffed. "I'm sorry I ever met you," she said bitterly. "You're mean and cruel and I hate you."

Lilly sighed as dismay sunk down into her belly. Astrid was lashing out, wanting to cause David the same degree of pain as she felt. After yesterday's wonderful night of happiness, this change of atmosphere was painful.

David slid his gaze from Astrid's and across to Lilly's, saying nothing with his lips because his eyes said it all. Astrid had proven that the faith he'd placed in her had been wrongly given. Her daughter had let David down and he was clearly taking it hard.

"She doesn't mean what she's saying," Lilly said. "She's hurting."

David remained silent, while Goldie twisted in her seat to reach around and pat Lilly's hand. Lilly was thankful of the gesture, but it made her frustration with David all the more intense. *He* should be the one providing comfort, not Goldie. Lilly thought they'd made a special connection, become a united front, but now their union had seemingly fallen apart.

"Why don't you say something?" she said, raising her voice. "Or are you going to now give me the silent treatment?"

"I'm thinking about where to go from here." David replied. "I need a plan."

The next words out of Lilly's mouth were a no-brainer. "I want to go home."

"There's no way you can go back to Oakmont," he said. "Henderson has already broken into your home and it's the first place he'll look for you when he finds out we're no longer in this area."

She repeated her request. "I want to go home. I want

to be in my own community, surrounded by people who love me and Astrid. Take us home, please."

"Lilly," he said, his eyes flitting between her and the glistening road ahead. "You can't be serious. Oakmont is the very worst place you can go right now."

"I'm not under arrest, right?" She was determined, exhausted and terrified, but she would not take orders from this man any longer. "I demand that you drive me home this instant."

David took his time to formulate a response. "I won't let you put yourself in danger like that, Lilly. I'll go to a rest stop while we organize another safe house."

"No!" Her shout caused Astrid to jump and Lilly rubbed her shoulder soothingly. "I'm prepared to face whatever comes our way because I have faith that we'll stay safe. If you won't take us home, I want you to stop this car right now and we'll get out and walk through the storm."

She knew David would never ever allow her to leave his protective custody, and this was her trump card. All she wanted was to tuck Astrid into her own bed surrounded by her childhood teddies and photos of her friends on the pin board. David might not be able to understand Lilly's reasoning, but she didn't care. In the darkest of times, home offered the most comfort.

"You two need to stop with the fighting," Goldie said, holding up a hand. "If this is what it means to fall in love, then I'm glad I'll never experience it." She turned to David. "If Lilly insists on going home, we're obliged to take her there. We'll stay with her until Henderson is captured." She looked between Lilly and David. "The tension between you guys is too much. Take it down a notch."

"I apologize," David said quietly. "Goldie's right. I'll take you home if that's what you really want. I'll get some security measures put in place to protect you and Astrid from attack and hopefully this will be over soon."

"It can't come soon enough," Lilly muttered under her breath.

She was done with this whole petrifying ordeal, with David and his stubbornness, with Henderson and his constant lurking presence. She was sick of running and if Henderson found her, she would fight him with her own bare hands if necessary.

The only help available to her now came from her faith. Even amongst the arguments and recriminations, the Lord remained steadfast, offering a sense of peace and serenity.

She put her hands together, closed her eyes and silently prayed for an end to this nightmare, for Astrid's safety and for David's anger to subside. As her lips mouthed the words, she felt Astrid tug on her arm, wanting to be part of the prayer her mom was making. Lilly smiled at her, took her hands and said the same prayer out loud, this time inviting a blanket of protection for each person in the car.

As the car's occupants said "amen" in unison, a roadblock came into view on the street that would take them out of the woods. A solitary police vehicle was parked behind a yellow barrier that displayed the sign Road Closed Ahead.

As David rolled to a halt, an officer exited the vehicle and walked toward them, hand on his gun and a peaked cap pulled low over his face.

"Can we turn around and go back the other way?" Lilly asked. "I've got a really bad feeling about this."

"I can't see this guy's features," David said. "It might be Henderson, but it could be a legitimate cop." He turned around to face Lilly. "Is this the guy who impersonated François Berger?"

"I don't know." She narrowed her eyes at the policeman in the poor visibility of the torrential rain. "It's hard to tell."

As the officer came to stand directly in front of their car, David activated the electric window and called out.

"What's the problem, Officer?"

"There have been reports of a gunman in the area," came the reply. "I want all occupants out of the vehicle, please."

"That won't be necessary," David said, pulling his badge from his jacket pocket and holding it out into the fat raindrops. "My name is David McQueen and I'm a federal agent. Let us pass."

The officer pulled his gun. "Get out of the car! Now!"

David put the SUV in reverse and began to back up fast, just as the bullets started to fly. The windshield shattered, sending tiny fragments sailing through the car. Lilly saw blood, didn't know whose it was and made a grab for Astrid. It was only when he yelled out in pain that she realized the blood was David's. He was injured, making a desperate attempt to take them away from a deranged killer.

Whatever animosity she felt toward him now had to be pushed aside, because her life was in his hands, along with that of her daughter. She had to trust him implicitly.

TEN

The car whined against its high speed in reverse, as David floored the gas pedal. Henderson had returned to his stolen patrol car and was pursuing their vehicle, gaining with each second. Soon they were nose to nose, Henderson firing erratically through the driver's window. His bullets were off target, pinging past the car somewhere beyond Lilly's vision as she cowered in the back seat, covering Astrid as much as possible.

"We'll be fine, honey," she whispered to her daughter. "Keep down low."

"This is all my fault," Astrid whimpered. "He found us because of me."

"Don't think about that now. Just focus on staying out of sight."

In her peripheral vision, she saw Goldie kicking the windshield with her feet, trying to dislodge the shattered glass. But it was tough and wouldn't budge, so Goldie leaned through her window to provide return fire, and each time her weapon discharged a bullet, Astrid's whole body convulsed with the noise.

"Hold on!" David yelled. "I'm turning around."

He yanked the hand brake, spinning on the asphalt,

tires squealing. The turn meant that the car lost speed and the patrol car slammed into them from behind, sending Astrid and Lilly tumbling forward, stopped only by their seat belts.

David unclipped his radio, requesting immediate assistance at their location.

"I'll get us out of here," he shouted, pulling a sharp right. "There's another exit on this road."

"It's blocked," Goldie shouted. "Watch out!"

Lilly lifted her head to see a large motor home parked sideways across the road. Two cars had already stopped behind it, and their occupants were standing beside their vehicles in the rain, looking around for the absent driver. Henderson had obviously stolen the motor home in order to block the escape routes. As always, he'd planned ahead.

"I'm going off-road," David said, yanking the wheel to take them onto the grass. "I need to lead Henderson away from these people. Hold on to something."

Lilly only wanted to hold on to one thing—Astrid. Her daughter was shaking with fear and shame, knowing that their attack had resulted because of her naïveté.

The car bumped and bounced across the slushy grass, and Lilly struggled to keep hold of Astrid as her limbs jarred with the force. Goldie stopped firing, obviously concerned for the lives of those people on the road, and this gave Henderson a little more confidence to shoot at will. There was the sound of bang after bang. The back window shattered and a bullet lodged in the door frame above Lilly's head. She looked at it in horror, imagining the damage it could do to a human body.

"He's blown one of our tires," David said. "I'm going into the woods and we'll take cover there."

Lilly turned her head to look up out the window. Thick trees came into view, their foliage rushing past in a blur of green. The car twisted and turned without warning as David weaved through the woods, the blown back tire giving the car a strange lopsidedness.

Then there was a crash and Lilly was flung forward. Both airbags deployed in the front of the car, rising up with a hiss.

"We hit a tree," David shouted. "We'll have to shoot it out from here. Goldie, let's go." He glanced at Lilly, cowering in the back with Astrid. "Stay here, out of sight."

Then he was gone, leaving behind a crimson bloodstain on the upholstered seat. She heard shots being exchanged, lots of shouting and the hammering rain on the roof.

As a lull in the gunfire came, Lilly felt confident enough to peek above the seat to try to work out their proximity to danger. She saw David a few yards away shielded behind a tree, Goldie behind another, both reloading their weapons. But where was Henderson? The patrol car he'd been driving was positioned right behind their SUV, battered from the chase and entirely empty. Through the trees, in the distance, a team of uniformed officers was pushing the motor home from the road to allow a convoy of police cars to head their way, following the muddy tracks made by their tires. Help was coming, and perhaps Henderson had been scared off.

A movement caught her eye and she tracked it between the trees. It appeared to be a slow-moving bush, a pile of leaves and branches shuffling along the ground headed for their SUV. And sticking out the back of this bush was a pair of boots.

"Come on," she said to Astrid, opening the door as

her heart pumped with adrenaline. "We gotta get out of here."

Astrid was reluctant to move from their seemingly safe hiding spot. "No, Mom. David told us to stay here."

Lilly pushed her daughter from the car. "And I'm telling us to leave. Go!"

Astrid fell to the soggy ground with a squelch and Lilly dropped next to her, rain soaking through to her scalp in seconds. Then the bullets came from the opposite side of car, peppering the metal indiscriminately, one after the other. Lilly knew with surety that both she and Astrid would have been killed if they'd remained inside.

David appeared at her side, drawn by the bullets, the sleeve of his white shirt saturated with his blood. "Go take cover behind that tree," he said, pointing to a thick trunk. As the gunfire ceased, he tilted his head, hearing the building sirens. "Backup is here. We'll have him surrounded."

"That's what we thought last time," Lilly said, taking Astrid's hand and pulling her to the tree, where they both slid down the rough bark and clung to each other, hearing the police convoy move ever closer.

Goldie raced past, her red curls dripping wet, gun positioned and ready to fire. Within another few seconds the sirens flooded the woods, clashing with one other, until they ceased abruptly and a voice bellowed through the air.

"I want to see your hands in the air. Drop your weapons."

David's voice rang out in response. "We're both FBI agents on an assignment to protect two civilians who've been targeted for murder by a known con man."

Lilly crawled around the trunk as she saw Henderson

himself come into view, brushing wet leaves from his uniform, adjusting his peaked cap. Now that she could see him much closer, he was instantly recognizable as the man who had introduced himself as François Berger. Behind the false beard and eyeglasses, his freckled skin and icy blue eyes were seemingly innocent but powerfully chilling.

"Stay there," she whispered to Astrid. "I'll be right back." Then she stood up, pointed to the con man and shouted to the dozen or so officers surrounding David and Goldie. "Arrest him," she pleaded. "He's been trying to kill me."

"Put your hands up, ma'am," one of the officers called. "Do you have a weapon?"

Her hands shot into the air, reacting instantly to the order. "No, I don't have a gun. You have to believe me, please. This policeman is not who you think he is."

On hearing this, Henderson strolled over to the officer and casually spoke into his ear.

"This officer from Beaver County tells me he witnessed you people robbing a store in Beaver Falls and pursued you here after you failed to stop," the policeman said. "It's a crime to make a false statement to the police, so think carefully about what you're saying."

"It was me who requested backup," David said, his hands raised high and his gun on the ground. "You're responding to *my* call."

Henderson yet again spoke quietly into the officer's ear.

"Nice try, buddy," the policeman said to David with a smile. "But Officer David McQueen here made the call, not you."

"No," shouted David. "His name is Gilbert Henderson. *I'm* David McQueen. Check my badge. It's in my left pocket. You're making a huge mistake."

The officer was clearly affronted. "You're the one making the mistake. Whatever stunt you're trying to pull won't work with me. You're all under arrest."

"No, no," Lilly said. "He's getting away." She watched in dismay as Henderson ambled through the trees, making for the road. "You have to stop him."

The officer in charge was now in no mood to tolerate their protestations. "Officer McQueen is going to reassure those good people who were scared to death by your high-speed pursuit. Keep quiet and let him do his job."

Lilly could do nothing but stare in disbelief as her chance of freedom slipped away. The unfairness of it was staggering.

"My daughter is hiding behind the tree back there," she said, realizing that they were all out of options. "She's only fifteen years old, so please be gentle with her."

With each second, Henderson was walking out of reach, his ambling walk full of arrogance and smugness. As he reached the road, he turned, smiled and gave a wave, as if taunting them. Then he strode right past the people he was meant to be comforting and vanished into the woods beyond, behind the blanket of rain.

"We've lost him this time," David said, shaking his head. "But next time will be different."

Lilly wanted to cry. He was deluding himself. Not only was Henderson outsmarting them at every opportunity, but she and David were fighting over Astrid and disagreeing about where to go next. Henderson had escaped, everything had fallen apart and she was mentally exhausted.

Lilly intended to return home and request that David be replaced with another agent. It was painfully clear that she needed to call time on their relationship, both professionally and romantically.

David walked through Lilly's single-story home with a sinking heart. This house was a bodyguard's nightmare—three points of entry, plenty of dark corners in the yard and on a street wide enough to drive a tank down. They were facing a villain so cunning that David certainly didn't want to give him any advantages.

Lilly walked along the hallway, freshly showered, towel drying her hair and wearing her favorite blue sweat suit, the one that perfectly matched her eyes.

"I needed that hot shower," she said. "It's nice to be home."

After being held in a police station for an hour, they had all been glad to be released without charge when their identities had been established. Beaver Falls Police had also confirmed that one of their vehicles was stolen overnight along with a uniform in the trunk. David's superiors had given the arresting officers a stern rebuke for allowing a wanted man to escape so easily, but it would in no way compensate for the damage done. Thanks to their incompetence, Henderson remained a free man. The only upside to the latest incident was the inclusion of another charge on his arrest warrant: impersonating a police officer. For a man who usually left no evidence behind, Henderson's decision to reveal his face to so many people showed how desperate he had been to escape. And he would be furious about the forced error, possibly now giving him a personal score to settle with David, as well as a desire to eliminate Lilly as a witness.

"How's your arm?" Lilly asked, touching the bandage that was visible beneath David's shirt. "Is it sore?"

"It's fine. It's just a small cut from the flying glass but it sure created a lot of blood. I put the shirt in the trash."

She smiled. "At least it was only the shirt that was seriously hurt."

A silence fell, awkwardness yet again settling between them.

"How's Astrid?" he asked. "I haven't gotten a chance to talk to her yet."

"She's happy to be home," Lilly replied. "There's no other place we want to be right now."

He cast a gaze around them. "Listen, Lilly, this isn't an ideal location for me to protect you. I'd much rather you reconsidered your plan."

"You don't have to protect me," she said, wringing her hands. "In fact, I think I'd rather you weren't here at all."

"What?" He couldn't quite believe what he was hearing. "Goldie can't protect you and Astrid alone. That's not possible."

"I was thinking that you could organize a replacement," she said. "Somebody new who doesn't have the same history that we have."

His anxiety soared. His greatest fear was coming true. He was losing her. After wrestling with his feelings for what had felt like an eternity, he had finally overcome his doubts and let himself love Lilly. And now their relationship was crumbling, unable to withstand this test. Could he pull it back on track?

"You can't be serious." He reached for her hand, but she drew it from his grasp. "I know we had a fight but is it really worth throwing away what we have? We mean something to each other, right?"

"The way you treated Astrid after you found her with the cell phone was unforgiveable," she said. "She made a mistake and you tore a strip off her, even after she apologized."

"Somebody had to make her understand what she'd done." They had almost died numerous times because of Astrid's disobedience. "She never seems to learn."

"Yes, she does learn." Lilly was obviously exasperated. "Every time she makes a mistake, she grows from it, but you've gone and decided that she's a lost cause."

"I'm sorry, but I have a hard time trusting her after all the lies she's told and the disrespect she's shown. I thought she was growing up, but it was all just an act that totally fooled me."

"I've heard enough," Lilly said. "Astrid is in her room, feeling awful about what she's done and I refuse to let you punish her any more than she's punishing herself already. I want you to go."

"Nobody knows this case like I do." He locked eyes with her. "Nobody knows *you* like I do."

"Our relationship can't go anywhere, David," she said. "Not while you're unprepared to forgive Astrid."

"It's not a question of forgiving her," David protested. "It's about ensuring she doesn't have the ability to put us in danger again."

"And how do you suggest we do that?"

"By taking away access to all electronic devices, keeping a strict watch on her at all times and setting an alarm on her bedroom window to prevent Noah passing her another cell phone."

Lilly paced the hallway, crossing her arms and shaking her head. "I thought you'd changed but you've gone right back to the man you used to be."

He didn't know what she meant. "The man I used to be?"

"When we first met, you were determined to control Astrid's behavior by forcing her to bend to your rules and not allow her any freedom. But you two made a breakthrough when you started talking honestly to each other. I really hoped you'd begun to understand her, to see her as a young adult rather than nothing more than a rebellious child. It looks like I was wrong. You haven't changed at all."

This comment stung. David had changed and grown in character a lot since meeting Lilly and Astrid. He'd been made to understand that he'd pressured Chloe into seeking a career she hadn't wanted, and he'd let go of his past regrets in order to become a much humbler person. His desire to control Astrid now was a necessity to protect everyone in the house. She couldn't be trusted. Could she?

"Whatever has happened with Astrid doesn't change the way I feel about you," he said.

"Well, it changes the way I feel about you," Lilly shot back. "I explained to you that Astrid is my number one priority and if she hurts, then I hurt too."

"I'm just trying to keep you both alive," he said. "And sometimes I have to be tough. You can't make an omelet without breaking eggs."

Lilly let out a laugh, yet it wasn't one of genuine mirth. "Astrid's not an egg, David. She's a flawed, sensitive, maddening and bighearted young woman, who's been forced into a terrifying situation that she's not equipped for. Stop expecting her to have the coping mechanisms of an adult. Try and remember how it feels to parent a teenager."

He thought of Chloe and her determination to break the rules. At the time he hadn't seen the worry and pain that was causing the problem. He had focused on correcting her behavior, thereby only addressing the symptom and not the cause. And here he was again, making the same old mistakes. Maybe Lilly was right. Maybe he hadn't changed at all.

"I need you to help me see where I can improve," he said. "Because I know I get things wrong and I'm difficult to live with and I want to do better."

"I want you to tell Astrid that you trust her," Lilly said. "Do something that will build up her confidence and show her that you have faith in her again."

Lilly was asking too much. He wanted to have faith in Astrid, but he couldn't summon a sense of trust out of thin air. Keeping a secret cell phone, openly deceiving him and placing them in jeopardy were impossible actions to overlook.

"I'm not sure I can do that," he said. "I'm here to safeguard your lives, and that means making tough decisions."

"Yeah, you already told me," she said sarcastically. "You can't make an omelet without breaking eggs."

He sighed. They had reached an impasse, unable to find a way forward.

"You can stay here overnight," Lilly said, lifting her chin, apparently shoring up her defenses. "But I'd appreciate you organizing a replacement by tomorrow." David couldn't believe this was happening. What could he do to change her mind, to make her see that he only had her best interests at heart?

"Please listen to me, Lilly," he said, panic setting in at the thought of being banished from her forever. "This house is bound to come under attack sooner or later and I really, truly want to be here to protect you." This statement didn't go far enough to explain the depth of his feelings. "And I love you. I'd lay down my life for you and I can't promise that a replacement agent would do the same."

Her eyes became glassy and moist, and she blinked quickly. "You're a good man, David," she said. "But Astrid comes first, and she's already been rejected by her father. I won't let her be rejected by you too."

"I'm not rejecting her."

"Yes, you are," she said strongly. "You told her that she betrayed us. You called her immature and a bunch of other cruel things. If that's not rejection, then I don't know what is."

Hearing his own words thrown back at him made him realize how harsh they'd been. He thought they'd been necessary at the time but perhaps he had spoken too severely.

"Discipline is important," he said. "Otherwise, children will grow into adults who have no respect for anybody."

"Discipline without love is worthless," she said with sadness. "When God corrects us, He does it with kindness and understanding, teaching us that He still loves us in spite of our mistakes. We should do the same with each other."

This was undeniably true. "Do you think I disciplined Astrid without showing love?"

"Yes, I do, and I won't let you do it again. Organize a replacement and we'll take our chances with someone new." She continued her way along the hallway. "I'd like you to leave tomorrow."

David put his head in his hands. Lilly was the most determined and fierce she had ever been, her maternal instinct obviously pushed to the fore by the dressing down he had given Astrid. He had breached a boundary in a way that she wouldn't tolerate and her words had given him a lot to think about.

He had twenty-four hours to try to prove that he could be the man she wanted. Or face losing her forever.

Lilly found Astrid curled up on her bed, White Bear in her hands. So much for not needing him anymore.

"Hey," she said gently. "Is everything okay? You didn't have any lunch."

"I'm not hungry," Astrid replied. "And I'd rather stay in my room."

Lilly sat on the bed. "Are you avoiding David?"

"I let him down and I don't want to be reminded of it." She clutched White Bear closer. "The look in his eyes when he saw me with that cell phone was horrible, like he was so disappointed in me."

Lilly stroked Astrid's glossy hair. "You can see why he was disappointed though, right?"

"Sure I can. He probably hates me now."

"Oh, honey, he doesn't hate you. He cares about you and he likes you very much, but he thinks he has to be a tough guy to keep us safe." She rested her hand on Astrid's forehead, where a tiny scar sat on her temple, resulting from a fall as a toddler. Lilly knew every mark, every blemish, every freckle on her daughter's face. "I've asked him to leave and send a replacement agent to protect us. I think it's for the best."

Astrid sat up quickly. "You asked him to leave? Why did you do that?"

"Because he's making you feel bad about yourself. Because he isn't trying to build a bridge with you. Because he doesn't understand that you need just as much love as punishment."

"But you like him." Astrid picked some fluff from her teddy self-consciously. "In fact, I think you love him."

"But I love you more, honey." In truth, the thought of letting David go caused Lilly's belly to ache, but she didn't want Astrid to know that. "We'll manage just fine without him."

"Will we?"

"Sure. We manage without your father, don't we?"

"Yeah, but David isn't like Dad," Astrid replied. "He's different."

Lilly had thought David was different at one point, but he had ended up letting her and Astrid down. Given another opportunity, he might let them down time and time again, just like Rylan. They didn't need David in their lives. They had each other and that was enough.

Astrid fell silent, her expression betraying her abject sadness. Lilly patted her leg.

"The new agent will be just as protective," she said, trying to be positive. "I'm sure of it."

"I know, but I got used to David, and I kind of like him."

This was a real surprise. "Wow. I didn't expect this reaction. I thought you'd be pleased to see him go. This morning you said you were sorry you ever met him."

Astrid grimaced as if the memory were painful. "That's because of the look in his eyes, Mom. I couldn't bear the shame of what I'd done, so I wanted to hurt him. Does that make sense?"

"It makes perfect sense, honey."

"I didn't mean the things I said to him. I actually

think David is smart and funny. And I like the rules he sets for me."

This was an even bigger surprise. "Are my ears hearing you right? You actually like his strong discipline?"

Astrid squirmed a little, clearly uncomfortable with what she was about to say.

"When David said that I run rings around you, he was right." She looked at her mother sheepishly. "You let me get away with backchat most of the time. I've been rude to you and refused to go to church and I've even made you cry." She gripped Lilly's hand. "And I want you to know that I'm sorry about it. David made me see that I've been a brat sometimes."

Lilly wasn't sure whether to feel pride in her daughter's maturity or shame that her parenting had fallen short.

"I had no idea that you felt this way," Lilly said. "What exactly about David's discipline do you like?" If she knew the answer to this, maybe she could replicate it. "Try and explain."

"It's like a security blanket," she said. "Rules make me feel safer because I know that someone is concerned about me. David's rules feel like strong arms, hugging me tight, and I got used to them in the end. He's way too strict sometimes but then you step in and tell him to back off, so it works really well." She smiled. "I think you guys make a really great team."

"You do?"

"Yeah, I do, and I'm sad that I messed it all up. You're telling him to leave because of me."

Lilly reached out and pulled Astrid into a hug, cradling her head while Astrid cuddled White Bear.

"I'm telling him to leave because…" She couldn't remember why.

"Because he's stubborn and stiff and won't believe that I can be trusted." Astrid's laugh was hollow. "Am I right?"

"Yes," she said, refusing to laugh along. This was way too serious for that. "I will never allow any man into this family unless he adores you just as much as I do. You are a beautiful person who happens to make mistakes, exactly like everybody else."

"I just happen to make more mistakes than most," Astrid said. "But I'm trying hard to do the right things now. I really am."

Lilly kissed her forehead. "I know that, honey, and I'm proud of you for using this experience as a way to learn and grow."

"Thanks for bringing us home, Mom. I needed to be back in my own room."

Lilly's heart skipped a beat, and she hoped Astrid didn't notice the fear. Returning to her quaint little home in Oakmont was bittersweet. On the one hand, she was surrounded by familiar things, including her neighbors and friends, but on the other hand, she would be so easy to find. Henderson would have no difficulty in locating her here, the most likely place in the world.

And once David was gone, she could no longer rely on his protection. Much like Astrid, Lilly had gotten used to his strength and security, and losing his safe hands would be a wrench.

She would have to learn to be strong all on her own once again.

David stood on the sidewalk, scanning the street in both directions. All was quiet on this leafy street, lined with single-story homes, windows bright in the darkness. Directly outside Lilly's home was a patrol car with two officers inside.

Lilly approached, walking down the driveway, carrying a tray of mugs, each steaming in the cold air.

"Take one of these," she said, holding the tray toward David. "Goldie says you're on first shift tonight, so you'll need it."

He took it gratefully. "Thanks."

Lilly walked to the police car and waited for the window to slide down before offering the two officers the remaining mugs. They took them with a smile and waved their thanks. David had decided there was little point in trying to hide their presence here. It was better to have extra security and await the inevitable. As well as the lookout officers, a SWAT team was on permanent standby and could be mobilized within five minutes, giving him extra peace of mind.

Behind Astrid's drapes in her bedroom window there was a flicker of blue and green. She was watching television, having decided to spend almost all of her time on her bed.

"Astrid's avoiding me," he said. "She won't even look me in the eye."

"It's because she's ashamed of herself," Lilly said. "She can't face you."

David wasn't so sure. He reckoned it was more to do with her dislike of him and his strong rules. One thing Astrid definitely disliked was being constrained by rules.

"I'll miss her," he said sadly. "She's really gotten under my skin." He stared into his coffee. "Of course, it's nothing compared to the way *you've* gotten under my skin. I'll miss you more than I can ever explain."

"Astrid will miss you too," she said, ignoring the rest

of his sentence. "She actually likes you a lot. She thinks you and I make a good parenting team." Lilly smiled. She looked so tired. "Apparently you're too strong and I'm too soft, so we meet at a perfect point in the middle."

He returned her smile. "Like a sweet spot."

"I guess so."

David side-eyed her. "Astrid said that? She said she likes me?"

"Yes, she did. It's hard to believe she said it, but you know how contrary teenagers can be."

David was shocked at this revelation. He had assumed that Astrid was being deliberately standoffish and rude, refusing to engage with him because she wanted to rail against his authority. He hadn't stopped to consider that he might be wrong. And now it was almost too late to backtrack, because his replacement would be there in the morning. David would be officially transferred off the case at 9:00 a.m. tomorrow.

"Perhaps I should talk with her," he said. "What do you think?"

Lilly was hesitant. "I'm not sure. She's sad and vulnerable at the moment."

"And you're worried I might criticize her and make her feel even worse?"

Lilly nodded. "If you can't forgive her and trust her again, then leave her alone."

There was a hard edge to Lilly's words and he understood her ferocity perfectly. If somebody were to criticize Chloe for her bad choices, he would be as fierce in response. His daughter had accepted her mistakes with humility and didn't try to hide from them. Was it possible that Astrid had arrived at the same place as Chloe, ready to own up to her faults?

"I want to make things right between us, Lilly," he said. "I'll be removed from the assignment tomorrow morning as you wanted, unless you change your mind and I cancel the request."

"I don't know, David," she said. "It all depends on whether you can repair your relationship with Astrid. If you upset her, she'll become defensive and belligerent."

"I'm capable of exercising restraint," he said. "I have a light touch when I need it."

Lilly's faced showed skepticism, and again he understood why. He had come down hard on all of them over the last few days, demanding they unfailingly comply with all his rules. But now he felt differently. Now he wanted to change, to be more sympathetic and understanding, to be more like Lilly.

As he mulled these thoughts over in his head, the front door of the house opened, letting out a shaft of light onto the path, and Goldie stood in the doorway.

"Astrid says she hears noises and we're not sure where they're coming from," she called out. "Get inside. We need to go on lockdown."

ELEVEN

Lilly rushed into the house alongside David, and he bolted the door behind them. Astrid was standing in the hallway with Goldie, wearing fleece pajamas and fluffy socks, her eyes wide and worried.

"What did you hear, Astrid?" David asked, going into the living room to peek through the drapes. "Was it someone outside the window?"

"It was weird," she replied. "Like something was scratching inside the walls."

"Mice?" he suggested.

"No, it was too loud for mice."

Lilly went to her side and held her hand. "Squirrels perhaps?"

"Maybe, but it sounded too rhythmic to be an animal. I thought it was a person."

"Squirrels can make rhythmic sounds when they gnaw on things," David said. "And they can be loud too."

"I don't know what it was," Astrid said. "But it scared me."

"Where did you hear it?" he asked.

"In my room and here in the hallway. The noise seemed to be all around me."

David held a finger to his lips. "Let's all listen for it."

The four occupants of the house fell silent, ears slightly upturned, straining to hear. Lilly heard a dog bark in the distance, a siren on the highway and the whirr of the central heating, but nothing else.

"I didn't imagine it," Astrid said. "I definitely heard a noise."

David placed a hand on her shoulder. "I believe you, but it's gone now. Would you like me to check the attic as a precaution?"

Her face flooded with relief. "Would you do that?"

"Sure." He walked to the hatch and pulled the cord, sending the ladder sliding to the floor. "What do you keep up here, Lilly?"

"Christmas decorations, some old furniture, paints and brushes—the usual kind of stuff."

He took his gun from his holster and climbed the creaky ladder while Goldie held it steady. As soon as his head disappeared into the darkness, he called out, "I need a flashlight. I can't see a thing."

"There's one attached to the wall by the hatch," Lilly said. "Be careful, David. Some of the boards are a little rotten so tread carefully."

His legs vanished from sight and they heard his footfall overhead. Meanwhile, Astrid clung to her mother, her gaze raised toward the ceiling, following the creaky footsteps above her head.

David coughed. "It's dusty up here, but I don't see anything out of the ordinary."

"Does it look like anything has been disturbed?" Goldie shouted. "Take a good look."

"There are boxes, packed and stacked, suitcases in the corner, a folding table and chairs and... What's this?"

Lilly took a sharp intake of breath. "What is it?"

"I think it's a canoe."

She breathed out in relief. "Yeah, that's Astrid's. It was an old hobby of hers."

"Do you see any squirrels?" Astrid asked. "Or mice?"

He was silent for a few seconds. "No, but it looks like your boxes have been chewed on the corners, so that's likely the cause of the noise. You have rodents up here."

"That's great," Lilly said with a smile. "I never thought I'd be so relieved to have rodents in my attic."

They all listened as David's steps did another circuit of the boards, the beam of his flashlight bouncing around in the dark square of the attic entrance.

"I'm coming down," he said, his foot appearing on the top rung of the ladder. "And I might need to head straight for the shower."

As he emerged through the hole, Lilly saw that he was covered in dust, silvery threads of old cobwebs resting lightly on his brown hair and beard.

"You look like an old man," Astrid said with a laugh.

He shook his head, sending dust rising into the air, and Astrid helped to brush down his shirt, picking pieces of debris out of the collar.

"Mom, we really need to clean the attic," she said. "And get rid of the squirrels."

"I'll do that for you," David said. "I use humane traps to catch them and then release them in a park."

"I thought you were leaving tomorrow," Astrid said. "Mom says you've organized a replacement agent."

David glanced at Lilly. "Well, I can stay if you want me to."

Astrid shrugged, and Lilly recognized the gesture as defensive. Astrid was protecting herself against another fatherly rejection. "It's up to you," she said. "I don't care."

"That's not true, honey," Lilly said. "You care a lot."

Astrid folded her arms. "No, I don't. He can leave if he wants. I won't beg him to stay."

Lilly closed her eyes, wanted to weep for the amount of times Astrid had begged her biological father to come visit, only to be let down time and time again. Her daughter was expecting it to happen again, making the assumption that David would run out on her just like Rylan did. Lilly understood this fear perfectly.

"I'm here for you, Astrid," David said. "I want to apologize for the things I said this morning and I'm sorry for hurting you."

"You never hurt me," Astrid lied, her emotions rising. "So just pack your bags and leave us alone. You never cared about me anyway, did you? There's no need to pretend."

"I'm not pretending," he said calmly. "I care about you a lot."

"You're a liar!" she shouted, sudden and high-pitched. "You hate me."

David said nothing, and Lilly waited for his eventual reaction. Would he send Astrid to her room, demand submission, tell her she was disrespectful?

Instead of saying these things, he slipped his hand into Lilly's. "Let's talk this through together."

Astrid huffed, stormed to her room and slammed the door. Meanwhile, Lilly looked down at her fingers entwined in David's and wondered whether she could really, truly rely on him to be sensitive and kind, nurturing and fatherly. Could he be all of those things that Rylan was not?

With a big discussion in the cards, it looked like those burning questions were about to be answered once and for all.

David opened the door to Astrid's room slowly and found her lying facedown on her bed, her head buried in a pillow.

"Hey," he said, gently. "Can we come in?"

Astrid said nothing, so he led Lilly toward her bed and they both sat on the edge, hands clasped together, a joined force. This conversation had the power to make or break his future happiness and he needed Lilly's stabilizing influence to help him pitch it right. She was the softness to his strength, the gentle influence that would remind him to always speak with love.

"I have something to give you, Astrid," he said, slipping a cell phone from his pocket and placing it on the pillow. "I know you miss Noah a lot so I thought you might like to call him."

Astrid raised her head. "You're giving me a cell phone?"

"Yes, I'm giving you a cell phone. It's one of our special devices so the calls can't be intercepted, but I only want you to use it to call Noah. I know we're not officially in hiding anymore, but social media and emails are out of bounds, okay? Henderson might learn too much about the house and its weak spots, so it's best to have an internet blackout for now."

She sat up, wiped her eyes. "Aren't you worried?" she asked, picking up the cell and running her fingers over the numbers. "You remember what I did last time."

"I'm not going to lie to you," he said. "I am a little

worried, but I want to give you a chance to prove yourself. You can keep the phone in your room."

She put the cell on her bedside dresser. "I'll call Noah in the morning. He'll be really pleased to get an actual phone call instead of a Snapchat message." She dropped her eyes. "Thank you."

"You're welcome. Tell me about Noah. Does he treat you well? It's important that you hold him to a high standard because teenage boys can misbehave sometimes."

"Noah doesn't misbehave," Astrid said hotly. "He's really good to me."

Lilly squeezed David's hand. "I think what David is trying to say is that you only deserve the best, honey."

He smiled at Lilly, grateful that she was pulling him back on track. "That's exactly what I meant," he said. "You're a great person and I just wanted to check that Noah sees you in the same way."

"Oh, he does," Astrid said. "He says he wants to marry me one day."

He was incredulous. "You're only fifteen." Another squeeze of the hand came. "But it's nice that he's planning ahead."

"Noah says we can buy a house in Pittsburgh when we're married, and he'll teach in one of the public schools. He wants to be a science teacher."

"A science teacher, huh?" This reassured him. The same boy who was immature enough to give Astrid a secret cell phone was also sensible enough to choose to be an educator. "He sounds like a good kid."

"That's what I was trying to tell you when you met him," Lilly said with a laugh. "But it wasn't such a good time. His family attends the same church as me, and

Noah stops by every Sunday to ask Astrid if she'll go along with him."

Astrid made a face. "I don't like that church, Mom. It's so boring."

An idea pinged into David's mind. "Chloe just started going to a church youth group in Penn Hills. It's not too far from here if you'd like to give it a try. I can drop you off and pick you up. Noah too."

At this suggestion Astrid became animated. "I'd love to meet Chloe," she said. "She sounds super cool. Do you think she'd like me?"

"I think she'd love you," he replied. "You two have a lot in common. As soon as it's realistically possible, I'll drive you to Penn Hills and you and your mom can meet her together."

David glanced at Lilly, worried she would be irritated with him for making decisions without consulting her, but she was smiling, seemingly pleased at the way he was handling this conversation.

"I know we've both made mistakes in how we've dealt with you lately, Astrid," Lilly said. "I haven't disciplined you enough and David's discipline has sometimes been too tough, but you said yourself that we make a good team."

"And your mom is the better half," David said, kissing Lilly's hand. "By a long way."

"That's true," Astrid agreed. "But you're okay too."

David had had enough experience of teenagers to understand that being called okay was a huge compliment. But he wanted to go further.

"I want to be more than okay, Astrid," he said. "I hope to be someone that you admire and respect, and in order to achieve that I'll have to lay down some rules at times."

"That's okay," she said. "I like rules." She smiled. "Apart from the ones about homework. I hate those rules."

"Okay," he said with a smile, writing on an imaginary notebook with his finger. "No homework rules."

"If we're going to make this work, we have to be prepared for some tough times ahead," Lilly said. "And we have to agree to speak to each other in a loving way, even when we're angry or upset. We always speak the truth in love. Agreed?"

David recognized the words of Scripture as being from Ephesians. It was a perfect line of guidance for their situation.

"We speak the truth in love," he said, hand across his heart.

"We speak the truth in love," Astrid repeated after him, quickly adding, "apart from the truth about homework."

He laughed. "I get it," he said. "You hate homework. But I still want you to do it."

"Does this mean you're not leaving tomorrow?" Astrid asked hopefully.

David let go of Lilly's hand and stood up. "I'm not leaving tomorrow. I'll go make the call to cancel my replacement." He walked to the door, realized something, stopped and turned around. "I forgot to ask if that's okay with you both. This has got to be a joint decision, right?"

"I know I might not always show it, but I want you to stay," Astrid said. "What about you, Mom?"

Lilly smiled at him, long and lingering.

"I want you to stay too," she said. "I'm so glad we had this conversation."

"Me too." He looked around the room and raised his eyebrows at Astrid quizzically. "What happened to the huge mess that was in here a few days ago? I can see the carpet."

"I tidied up," she said. "I did a good job of it, huh?"

He dropped to his knees to peer at the space under the bed, only to see it crammed with her shoes, purses and books, jumbled together in a heap. As he burst into laughter, Astrid and Lilly did the same.

"Welcome to Astrid's version of tidying up," Lilly said. "It's not perfect but it's definitely effective."

"No comment," he said diplomatically, heading for the hallway.

THUMP! A noise sounded from overhead, right above Astrid's room.

David stopped dead in the doorway and reached for his gun, raising his head to the ceiling.

"What was that?" Astrid asked, jumping from the bed. "That's not a squirrel. No way."

THUMP! THUMP! THUMP!

David tried to track the sound, hoping to pinpoint its exact location in the attic. Perhaps he could shoot through the ceiling, but without knowing what he was shooting at, he would run the risk of killing someone or something entirely innocent.

Goldie came running into the room. "Do you hear that?" she asked breathlessly. "It's in the attic."

"Stay with Lilly and Astrid while I take a look."

He raced to the hatch, pulled the cord and yanked down the ladder, flitting up the steps in a matter of seconds. Activating the flashlight, the yellow beam picked out Astrid's old canoe, bouncing along the floor, its front end rising up and thumping on the boards with huge force. For a second or two, he had no idea what was happening or how this yellow fiberglass boat could be moving entirely of its own accord. Then he saw a hand extend from the opening, someone making a desperate attempt to free themselves.

It was Henderson. He had somehow squeezed himself into the narrow space to successfully hide from view and was now apparently stuck. He must've been there since they arrived this afternoon, waiting for an opportune moment to strike.

David aimed his weapon, shouted, "It's over, Henderson. You're under arrest."

But the canoe's front end rose up one more time and came crashing down on one of the rotten boards with such force that it gave way with a huge crack. Both the canoe and David fell through the floor as more boards collapsed under the strain. He hit the carpet of Astrid's bedroom with a thump while suitcases and boxes came crashing on top of him, knocking his gun from his hand and winding his gut. In the commotion were screams and shouts, Goldie yelling that she was trapped beneath a fallen bookcase. Lilly called out David's name and he bellowed a response from beneath the pile of her belongings.

"Get out of the house! Go now!"

He punched the boxes and cases from his body, snatching up his gun and jumping to his feet to free Goldie. Upon lifting the bookcase, it was immediately apparent that his partner's leg was broken, and she was gritting her teeth against the pain.

"Go find Lilly and Astrid," she said. "Where's Henderson?"

He spun around to locate the canoe, seeing it resting in the corner, cracked into large pieces by the impact.

And Henderson was nowhere in sight.

* * *

Lilly ran for her life, pursued by the man who was determined to kill both her and her daughter. She fumbled to open the front door when a gunshot rang out, splintering the door frame above her head.

"Help us," she yelled, dragging Astrid down the path toward the patrol car at the curb. "Please help us."

Both officers leaped from the car, weapons drawn. As the sound of multiple gunshots cracked the air, Lilly ran for cover, pulling Astrid alongside her. She headed down the side of the house, taking the path that led to the back lawn, where she hoped to jump the fence into Mr. Peters's yard.

Glancing back, she saw the two officers slumped on the street, one lying motionless on the ground, the other leaning against the bumper of the patrol car, with a dark bloodstain spreading rapidly on his shirt. Their handguns had clearly been no match for the weapon in Henderson's hand.

The officer looked up, caught her eye. "Go!" he yelled, a grimace of pain on his face. "Get out of here."

But the officer's shout had only served to give away her and Astrid's position, halfway to the backyard, flattened against the fence. In an instant, Henderson came into view on the front lawn, wearing a bulletproof vest and holding a small but powerful submachine gun at his side.

And then his eyes locked with hers, pinning her to the spot like a rabbit in headlights. He held her gaze for a full two seconds, sending terror cascading from the top of her head to the tips of her toes. He had dropped his disguise entirely, and she saw his wickedness and savagery come pouring out. He seemed almost inhuman.

He smiled at her, a vile and terrifying smile that might be the last thing she ever saw.

"Lilly!" David's voice cut through her immobility. "Where are you?"

Henderson spun on the spot and sprayed bullets at the front of her house.

"Come on, Mom." Astrid was pulling her arm. "Let's go."

Lilly snapped out of her trance and raced to her backyard, wondering if David was okay. She had already seen a bookcase fall onto Goldie from the collapsed attic, so that meant he was battling alone.

"Jump over the fence, Astrid," she said, making a platform with interlocked fingers. "Quickly!"

Astrid placed her slippered foot onto her mother's hand and scrambled up the fence, swinging her long legs over the top and landing heavily on the other side. Lilly stood on tiptoes to peer over.

"You okay, Astrid?" she said, seeing Mr. Peters appear through his back door, confusion and fear on his face. "Go inside with Mr. Peters and wait for the police. A SWAT team will be here soon."

Mr. Peters rushed over and helped Astrid to her feet. "Aren't you coming too, Lilly?" he asked. "I don't know what's going on over there, but it sounds like you're better off on this side of the fence."

Lilly listened to the sound of the popping bullets from the submachine gun. The gunfight meant that David was still alive, holding off Henderson to distract him from reaching her and Astrid.

"I have to go help somebody," she said. "Please look after Astrid until more police officers arrive. I'll be back as soon as I can."

Tears fell down her daughter's face. "I want to stay with you, Mom. Let me come with you."

"I need you to do something far more important," Lilly said, blowing her a kiss. "I need you to pray for me and David and Goldie, okay? I love you."

Then she turned and ran to her back door, fumbling with the set of keys she always kept in her pocket. Finding and inserting the correct key required both hands due to the violent trembling, but she finally stumbled into her kitchen, breathing heavily, knowing that she had to find a weapon. Quickly.

Swallowing away her fear, she walked into the hallway, telling herself that she was fierce and brave, that she wasn't reckless or foolish for returning to the danger zone. Astrid was safe and that was the most important thing right now.

Lilly stopped in her tracks as the gunfire ceased. While Henderson had been firing bullets in the front yard, at least she'd known where he was. If she couldn't hear him, he could be anywhere. And she still needed a weapon. She headed straight for Astrid's room, hoping Goldie could help.

"Lilly!" Goldie exclaimed on seeing her. "You should be with David. What are you doing inside?"

Lilly cast her eyes quickly around the room, which was covered in debris and broken furniture, boxes and dust. Goldie lay amongst the mess, holding her bloodied leg, which was bent at an awkward angle and clearly causing her discomfort.

"I don't know where David is," Lilly said, dragging a bookcase across the floor and positioning it between Goldie and the collapsed door, then adding other items in an attempt to make a barricade. "And I have no idea where Henderson is either. I'll make a defense barrier for you and then I have to go find David. Do you have a spare gun?"

"Sure, but why do you need it?" Goldie said, wincing as she tried to reposition her leg. "Where are the cops from the patrol car? They're meant to hold off an attack until the SWAT team arrives."

Lilly shook her head, thinking of the blood that streaked the sidewalk. "They got shot."

"Take this," Goldie said, giving Lilly a handgun. "It has only twelve bullets in the chamber so use them wisely."

Lilly took the gun, her hand still trembling, and prepared herself for the terror that she was about to walk into.

"Wait," Goldie said, grabbing her sleeve as she went to stand. "Listen."

The back door was opening, the unmistakable creak of the hinge echoing from the kitchen. Goldie brought her fingers to her lips and motioned for Lilly to take up a defensive position behind her barricade.

"This might be Henderson," she whispered. "Wait here until he shows himself and then shoot. I can't get a good aim with my leg like this, so you'll have to take the lead."

Lilly's insides were awash with sickness and dread. She had returned to the house in order to assist David and she was failing. She wanted to guard Goldie, but David might need her assistance just as badly. Where was he?

Both Lilly and Goldie remained utterly silent while footsteps sounded in the hall. Doors were being opened before a spray of bullets exploded in the silence. Henderson was shooting up each and every room, hoping to drive her out. Lilly held her breath, felt her head grow dizzy and forced herself to breathe slowly and quietly. Henderson was almost at the door of Astrid's room.

The barrel of his gun came first, poking around the door frame, gray and metallic, pointed toward the wall. Goldie saw it too and grabbed Lilly, yanking her down just in time to avoid the spray of random bullets. They hit the carpet together, covering their heads as glass from the window rained down.

Finally, when the noise ceased, Lilly raised her head, shaking off the glass. David was standing directly behind the broken window, pushing the remaining shards though the frame with the butt of his gun. Blood streaked his face, neck and shoulder, soaking the cotton of his white shirt.

"He's reloading," David said, scrambling through the window to crawl to her side. "We don't have much time."

"You're hurt," she said.

"It's nothing—just a little bullet." He kissed her full on the lips. "Where's Astrid?"

"She's safe."

"Good. The SWAT team is less than two minutes away. We have to hold off Henderson until then, but he has an Uzi so it won't be easy."

Henderson perhaps heard these words because his next gun attack was the fiercest yet, probably spurred by the knowledge that he was less than two minutes away from facing a team of armed specialists who would be armed with the kind of weapons to counteract his machine gun.

His bullets sprayed the entire room, while its three occupants lay flat on the floor behind the makeshift barricade that was crumbling and splitting under the barrage.

"I see his feet," Lilly said, catching a glimpse of his black boots through a gap beneath the bookcase. "He's right by Astrid's teddy bear shelf." She recognized the flower doodle on the lower part of the wall, made by Astrid in permanent marker when she was eight years old. "We can get a good shot."

But no one could hear her above the noise of Henderson's machine gun. David was belly down, gun poised and ready to take action as soon as a lull in the gunfire occurred.

When that lull came, Lilly was the first on her feet, the first to take aim, the first to fire a shot. And her shot was bang on target, hitting Henderson in the back of the neck as he fled through the door while reloading. That one bullet was enough to send him falling to the floor, clutching his neck with his hand as the blood flowed through his fingers.

Lilly remained in her defensive position, wide stance, gun outstretched, her heart thundering in her chest. The one thing she had learned about Gilbert Henderson was that you never assumed he was defeated.

The room fell deathly silent as Henderson made a futile attempt to crawl into the hallway, but was apparently unable to use his legs. Lilly's bullet seemed to have caused paralysis and she found herself strangely pitying him as his breathing grew ragged and his coloring turned waxy. She stepped over the barricade intending to see to his wounds, but David pulled her back, put his arm around her shoulders.

"There's nothing you can do for him now. He chose this end."

Soon Henderson's ragged breathing became a rattle before fading out entirely, and for a few seconds, Lilly felt the breeze through the window and allowed the silence to wash over her. It was over. She was finally free of violence, and the tranquility that had been left in its wake was beautiful.

David spoke into his radio, giving the news to the SWAT team that the suspect had been neutralized but medical assistance was required for injured law enforcement. Then he lifted a sheet from Astrid's bed, laid it over the still figure of Henderson and moved his lips in silent prayer. As the sirens stopped outside her home, David drew her into his arms, holding her tight, inhaling deeply.

"You are awesome," he said. "The way you took Henderson down was incredible."

"I figured that if he got me first, then you'd take care of Astrid." Lilly knew with certainty that David would go to the ends of the earth not only for her, but also for her daughter. "She can rely on you."

David had proven himself to be the man she'd wanted her whole life. Until now, Lilly had always assumed she'd once loved Rylan, but the depth of affection she felt for David made her realize that she'd never truly experienced love before. Not like this.

He brought a hand to her face. "You can both rely on me. Always."

She smiled. "I think I love you."

He raised his eyebrows. "You *think*?"

"Okay. I *know* I love you." There was no need to be cautious anymore. "I really love you."

"Me too."

He weaved his fingers into her hair, wincing with the movement of his arm.

"You're in pain," she said. "You need to get to the

hospital. And so does Goldie. I see paramedics outside, so we should go to them."

"You know what's a natural pain relief," he said with a smile. "Kissing someone you love."

"Well, that's no good for me," said Goldie from her position on the floor. "I guess I'll just have to stick with the medical drugs."

"I'm very fortunate to have access to the best pain relief in the world," David said, leaning forward to touch noses with Lilly. "No drug could ever make me this happy."

Lilly closed her eyes and allowed the stress of the last few days to be released from her body as she kissed the man who had shown her what it meant to be in a good and loving partnership. In David's arms, she had finally found her other half.

EPILOGUE

David opened the door to Lilly's home with a spring in his step. It was Saturday night and he had booked a table at a fancy restaurant in Oakmont for a special date with Lilly. This evening he had planned to ask her a very important question.

"Hey, Astrid," he said, seeing her sprawled on the rug in the living room, head in her sketchbook, drawing cartoon characters. "I brought Chloe with me."

Astrid raised her head, broke into a huge smile and jumped up from the floor.

"Hi, Chloe," she said, enveloping his daughter in a hug. "I didn't know you were coming over."

Chloe held up a batch of photographs in one hand and a large album in the other. "I finally got around to developing a bunch of photographs from your sixteenth birthday party," she said. "I thought we could make an album of the best ones." She handed the album to Astrid and rifled through the photos to find a specific one. "This is my favorite." She was holding an image of her and Paul alongside Astrid and Noah, each of them beaming at the camera. "It was such a fun party. I loved it."

"It was the best party ever," Astrid said. "But I've

never made an actual photo album before. Do people still do that?"

David laughed. "Yes, Astrid, people still do that. I think an album would be a great keepsake. It captures the night when the Olsens and McQueens all got to know each other." He ruffled her hair. "And we've never looked back, huh?"

She smiled. "Not for a second. Thank you for organizing it, David. You did a great job and the music was surprisingly cool."

"That was because Dad asked me to make a playlist," Chloe said. "And I knew we'd like the same things."

David had pulled out all the stops to make Astrid's party the best it could be, especially as she and her mom had been forced to leave their home while it underwent repairs. He had rented a local community hall and almost given himself a heart attack blowing up hundreds of balloons with Lilly. But it had been worth it, and Astrid had thanked him a thousand times.

"Where's your mom?" he asked. "Our reservation is at seven."

Astrid gave him the side-eye. "Mom has been getting ready for two hours. What's so special about this date anyway?"

David wondered whether Lilly had an inkling of what he was planning. He was hopeless at hiding his feelings where she was concerned.

"I have *not* spent two hours getting ready," Lilly said, breezing into the room wearing a black dress and nude heels. "It's only been an hour and a half." She kissed Chloe on the cheek. "Thanks for coming to keep Astrid company, Chloe. She talks about you constantly. And she adores the church you both go to in Penn Hills."

Chloe linked arms with Astrid. "That's good because it just wouldn't be the same without her."

"You look amazing," David said, drawing Lilly into an embrace and breathing her vanilla scent. "I've been so nervous."

"Nervous?" Astrid said. "It's just a date, right? No need to be nervous."

David reached into his pocket and fingered the small black box nestled there. It contained a diamond engagement ring chosen with help from his eldest daughter, Sarah.

"It's none of your business why David is nervous, Astrid," Lilly said, wrapping a shawl around her shoulders. "Don't pry."

"Of course it's my business, Mom," Astrid said. "If David is going to propose tonight, then you'll end up being Lilly McQueen soon and I'll be the only Olsen in the family."

David hadn't considered this. Astrid was right. It wouldn't be fair to leave her on the periphery of the family.

"Well, your mom could choose to keep her surname if we end up getting married one day," he said. "And then you wouldn't be the only Olsen."

"Why can't I be a McQueen like you guys?" she asked. "I can change my name too, right?"

David found a sudden rush of emotions overwhelming him. He had never imagined that Astrid would actively choose to take his surname, to fully embrace his family as if it had always been her own.

"Would you really like that, Astrid?" Lilly asked. "You'd be happy to change your name?"

"Sure I would." She smiled at Chloe. "And then we'd be like real sisters."

"Awesome," Chloe said. "We can borrow each other's clothes."

"You do that already," David said with a laugh. He gave Astrid a playful punch on the chin. "Thanks for the support. I'm honored." He held up his hands, palms forward. "Although I haven't proposed yet, so this is all hypothetical."

Lilly pushed him to the door. "Enough talking. We'll be late for our reservation."

He opened the door to the summer's evening, seeing the blooming flowers in the yard and the manicured lawn, marveling at how beautiful Lilly's house looked now compared to the devastation wreaked by Henderson. David had pitched in to help every spare moment, rebuilding her home to make it even better than before.

Lilly took his hand while they walked down the path and he beeped his car to unlock it.

"You can just ask me now if you like," she suddenly blurted out. "I'm too excited to wait."

He feigned innocence. "I have no idea what you mean."

"You're going to propose tonight." She hopped from foot to foot like a child on Christmas. "But I don't think I can wait, so just ask me now."

He held open the passenger door. "I like to do things correctly," he said, thinking of the cake and sparklers that the waiter had been instructed to bring out on his signal. "I'm an old-fashioned guy."

She laughed. "Boy, you really are a stickler, aren't you?"

He raised an eyebrow. "I've been called worse."

They smiled, both remembering the difficult times of just a few months ago, when David had been a lot more rigid and unyielding than he was today. Lilly's support meant that he was much better equipped to deal with Astrid and her roller coaster of emotions these days. Astrid remained challenging at times, pushing her boundaries, causing his hackles to rise. But their family commitment to speak to each other only in love had reaped huge rewards and Astrid was growing in maturity and character with each passing day.

Lilly kissed him on the nose. "I promise to only ever call you strong and handsome and smart from now on."

He slid an arm around her waist. "And I promise to only ever call you perfect."

"Nobody's perfect," she said. "Not even me."

He planted his lips on hers for a good long while. "But you're perfect for me."

* * * * *

*If you enjoyed this thrilling story
from Elisabeth Rees,
watch for Goldie's book later this year.*

*Find more great reads at
www.LoveInspired.com*

Dear Reader,

Thank you for joining David and Lilly on their romantic journey. I hope you enjoyed reading their story as much as I enjoyed writing it. Parenting teens is a subject close to my heart, as I have one teenager of my own, and one in training. It's often hard to know how to manage teenagers' ups and downs, coupled with their constant demands. It is the perfect subject matter for a strong conflict between two people.

David and Lilly are both stubborn when it comes to accepting criticism of their parenting. Yet none of us is perfect. There is no faultless way to raise a child, no model parent and no foolproof way to avoid the pitfalls. It took Lilly and David a little while to work this out, but once they began adhering to the principle of speaking the truth in love, they let go of the idea of perfection and focused instead on simply enjoying the ride.

God only ever speaks to us in love, even when He is reprimanding us, and if we try to do the same with our own children, we cannot go far wrong.

Please join me for Goldie's story in my next book. I would love to welcome you as a reader again.

Blessings,
Elisabeth